A PINCH OF PASSION

a Recipes for Love novel

KELLY COLLINS

Chapter 1

Someday, someone will look at me like I'm everything they've been searching for their entire life...

That was the entry Allie Parks had written in her planner on January first when all responsible people wrote down their wishes and dreams ... right after they planned their year and outlined their professional goals. Possibly after highlighting monthly meetings and putting in daily accountability targets. As the chief operating officer of Luxe Resorts, she had little wiggle room for failure.

She sat at a corner table in the dining room and glanced around the space. It was an upscale lodge with high-timbered ceilings, antler chandeliers, and wood inlay walls depicting all the major mountain peaks in Colorado.

She flipped through the pages until she reached June and checked off the items she'd accomplished that morning. She might not have found her prince, but she'd resolved the linen problem. She touched the frayed table-cloth and heaved a sigh of relief.

At Wharton School of Business, she had a professor who never stopped talking about the Pareto Principle and how it held for almost everything in life. But it didn't work here in Timberline, Colorado. She'd exhausted eighty percent of her time and energy to get twenty percent satisfaction rather than the other way around. Still, at least it was resolved—no more see-through towels, threadbare sheets, or frayed table linens.

She'd resolved it with good old greenbacks. In her experience, most people were motivated by money, and Starr Linens wasn't an exception. They'd dug in their heels until a lucrative deal was settled. It was more than she hoped but less than she was willing to pay.

"Negotiating linen costs is not the hill I want to die on." She checked that item off her list and looked up from the dining table just in time to see her brother, James, lead his girlfriend, Danielle, through the Lodge. It was the restaurant Allie hoped would earn enough accolades to put them on the culinary map.

While linens were necessary, food was tantamount to success. A Luxe resort wasn't luxe if the food wasn't Michelin star worthy.

"Ah, new love…" she sighed as they approached, holding hands. "I'd settle for old love. Hell, I'd settle for any love."

"It sounds like time for a trip to Heartbeat," Danielle turned to James. "This time, you're invited."

Allie laughed. She was glad Danielle and James had worked out their differences and realized their love was the only truth they needed to know. Before seeing her brother with Danielle, she wouldn't have believed there was a perfect love for anyone, but James was genuinely happy he'd found "the one."

James pulled out Danielle's chair and took the seat next to her. "Wouldn't matter. You're my girls, and I protect what's mine." He leaned over and kissed Danielle square on the lips.

Allie stuck her finger in her mouth and mimicked gagging. "Really? You're torturing me with your love." She wasn't generally a busybody, but after James and Danielle broke up, she played her hand at being cupid just once, and it seemed to work out. She'd lured them both to Heartbeat, the hottest new club for pickups, and then disappeared, leaving them to figure it out on their own.

Her phone rang, and she pointed to her screen. "Sorry, but I have to take this if we intend to serve food at the resort." She jumped up and walked around the corner into a private dining room.

"Allie Parks," she answered.

For the next ten minutes, she heard every reason, from out of stock, to out of season, for why she couldn't have what she wanted when she wanted it.

"How much is it going to cost me?" she asked.

The man on the other end spouted off a ridiculous percentage increase.

"Not on your life. I'll pay three percent and the expedited delivery charges. Take it or leave it." She hated it when people thought they could bulldoze her. She might have been petite at five-foot-three, but she had the inner strength and fortitude of a T-Rex.

She hung up and headed back to the table. The *clickety-clack* sound of her heels against the tile flooring echoed through the almost empty dining room.

"Sorry about that." She checked off another item and closed her planner. "We've squared away on linen and produce."

Danielle, or Dani as her brother had nicknamed her, bounced in her seat. "That's wonderful news. How did you get the linen guy to consent?"

Allie sat up in her chair and smiled. "I told him I'd meet him in the alleyway on delivery days for a quickie."

James's jaw dropped open, and Dani cocked her head.

"Kidding. I offered him more money. Obviously, I hit the sweet spot, or I drove him batshit crazy, and he agreed to the deal to get rid of me." She picked up her planner and stuffed it into her bag. "How about lunch?"

No sooner had she sat down when Flynn, the kitchen manager, walked out with a bottle of red wine.

"Good afternoon. Thanks for coming in to sample the new menu. I've paired today's choices with a nice dry red." He poured a splash into James' glass and waited for his approval. James swirled and took a drink before passing the glass to Dani.

After a sip, she said, "It's not Pride Reserve, but it's better than boxed wine."

When he went to pour Allie a glass, she shook her head. "None for me; I've got to hit the road soon." A feeling of giddiness welled up inside her. "I'm looking at a place to live since I don't have a boyfriend I can crash with." She eyed her brother, who'd recently abandoned living with her at their father's vacation home, to move in with Dani. "I need to get out of Dad's house. It's too big and lonely to stay in all by myself."

"You can move into the little apartment attached to my office until you find something," Dani offered.

James shook his head. "No, she can't." His eyes pleaded with Dani. "Sometimes, that's the only place I can go to steal a kiss from you."

Allie watched her brother and Dani interact. They were two halves to a whole. Would she ever find her perfect half, or was she relegated to a life alone?

Flynn's sous chef, Mollie, arrived with the starter and set the tiny plates in front of them.

"To start, we have wild salmon tartare with sungold tomatoes, haricot vert, and pressed cucumber with a tomato consommé."

"Fancy," Allie said and took a bite. "It's good, but what sets it apart from Timberline's other fine dining experiences?"

Mollie laughed. "There are no fine dining experiences in Timberline. You have to cross into Aspen for that."

"True," James offered. "But what makes us different from anyone within a hundred-mile radius?"

Mollie stood taller and pressed her hands down the front of her blinding white chef's jacket. "Everything is organic. We purchase locally when we can. Just wait until you get to the main course. I've got a venison steak that will melt in your mouth."

"Oh good, wild game." Allie smiled and tried not to look like she might get sick. She'd rather eat canned pet food than gnaw on a piece of venison. It didn't matter how it was cooked; deer meat never tantalized her taste buds.

"I'll be back in a few minutes with the second course," Mollie said.

As soon as she was gone, Allie reached for her bag. "Sorry to eat and run, but I've got to get to the place I'm trying to buy."

"Where is it?" James pushed away his nearly empty plate.

"It's off of Pine Bluffs in a building called Evergreen. Get ready because it will need some of your magic." Her brother was a master craftsman and had the skills to turn a piece of coal into a diamond in record time.

He pointed at her. "Are you wearing that?"

She stood and looked down at her Chanel suit and Louboutins. "What's wrong with the way I'm dressed?"

"Nothing." He shook his head. "Just hand over your checkbook and let the realtor write in the amount she wants. You can't negotiate a fair price when your shoes probably cost more than her mortgage."

He had a point. Allie glanced at her watch. If she hurried, she could return to her father's and change into something nice but didn't say empty my bank account.

"You're right. I'll change and then head over."

"Take Dad's old Jeep instead of the Porsche."

"You make me sound awful with your brand shaming."

He shrugged. "No use arriving with a neon, flashing dollar sign that says I can pay whatever you ask."

"Whatever." She dismissed him with a wave of her hand. "You two be good," she said, moving past them. "Let me know if the menu is up to par."

* * *

She rushed home. As she approached the house, she laughed. Her father, who spent his summers on the golf course in Palm Springs, called it their winter cabin, but it was twelve thousand square feet of pure luxury, not the tiny stacked log structure that the word cabin implied. He kept the place only because her mother didn't get it in the divorce, and it was paid for.

She raced inside and changed into black slacks, a pink silk blouse, and Kate Spade loafers. She refused to dress down completely. There had to be an entry point to the multimillion-dollar building, and she didn't want to appear underqualified either.

The little detour to change her clothes put her behind schedule. She climbed into her father's old Jeep. Old wasn't entirely accurate. It wasn't even out of warranty, but it had seen some four-wheeling and had a road-hard look about it with its scarred rims and dented quarter panel.

She whipped down the long winding driveway and turned onto the highway. She could make up a few minutes and be on time if she pushed the limits. Someone once told her that early was on time, and on time was late. Though she always had a lot on her plate, respecting other people's time was critical.

Reaching to grab the lipstick in her purse, she

swerved and slightly crossed over the line. The car coming her waylaid on the horn and offered an unpleasant gesture. She overcorrected, sending the Jeep into a fishtail and causing her heart to skip a beat at the near miss.

"No shade of red is worth dying over." She took a few deep calming breaths, but her Heartbeat jolted when she saw the flashing red lights in the rearview mirror.

"Not now." She mentally counted her most recent ticket and wondered how many points she could lose on her license and still be allowed to drive. "How fast was I going?" she asked out loud. She looked down at the speedometer and realized she was traveling nearly twenty miles over the limit, which was a six-point ticket. "I'm so screwed."

She slowed down and pulled to the side of the road. A thousand thoughts went through her mind, but the loudest was, *how can I get out of this mess?*

In the mirror, she watched the officer in the cruiser behind her. She knew how this went. He'd sit there a few minutes and make her sweat. Undoubtedly, he'd run the plates to be sure the car wasn't stolen. She said a silent prayer hoping the registration was up to date.

She considered her options as she waited for the officer to stroll to her window. She could cry, but the officer handed her a Kleenex and a ticket the last time she did that.

She could undo another button on her blouse and try to woo him out of a citation, but most chickens had bigger breasts than she did.

She could say it was a bathroom emergency, but

dysentery was no joking matter. When they'd been looking at a site in Mumbai, she experienced food poisoning. It was one of the reasons they didn't take over the property. The restaurant had been closed several times for health violations, and the resort would never recover from having the reputation of making people sick. Nope, she wouldn't lie about a bathroom issue.

She considered using humor, but the only police officer joke she knew was, *What do you call it when a prisoner takes his own mug shot? A cellfie.* That would probably get her thrown in jail for having criminally lousy taste.

She could fake sick and say she was on her way home to rest, but if he looked at her driver's license, it would show an address in Breckenridge which was precisely the opposite direction she was heading.

Note to self ... update the address on my license.

She could be honest.

She watched as the officer climbed out of his cruiser. He was tall, dark, and deadly, or at least his expression was. This was going to be bad—really bad.

Chapter 2

Officer Marco Rossi watched the Jeep fly past him. His handheld radar gun clocked the SUV going seventy on a fifty mile-per-hour stretch of highway. When he ran the plates, they belonged to an Alistair Parks. In his experience, a name like Alistair came with a big bank account and an attitude to match.

He kept his right hand close to his sidearm as he approached the driver's window. These days, he couldn't be too careful. Crime had no address, and even though he worked in Aspen, they had their share of problems.

He saw her reflection in the side mirror. This was no Alistair unless her parents had been hoping for a boy and went with the name, anyway. Sitting behind the wheel was a drop-dead gorgeous redhead—probably Alistair's trophy wife.

He moved to the driver's window, which she'd already rolled down. "Good afternoon, are you in a hurry?"

She pulled her lips into a smile. It wasn't a natural

one, but a smile that forced itself on her face. He couldn't blame her; she was getting a ticket, and that never brought joy to anyone. In all his years in law enforcement, he'd never been thanked for a citation.

"Was I speeding?" She batted her lashes.

"If you don't know how to read the speedometer, you probably shouldn't be driving. You were going seventy."

Her eyes grew wide. "Surely, I wasn't going that fast. I mean, that's twenty over the speed limit. A girl could lose her license for that."

"It would appear you're familiar with the penalties." He glanced inside the Jeep. It was tidier inside than outside. The mud-caked rims looked like she'd taken the SUV for a jaunt in the woods. "I'll need your license, registration, and proof of insurance, please."

She let out a heavy sigh and reached into the glove compartment to get the paperwork. She spilled her bag onto the front seat and rummaged through the mess to find her wallet.

For a woman who, at first glance, seemed put together, she appeared disorganized or at least ruffled. A book on her seat caught his eye. On the front was a large heart with the words *Recipes for Love*.

She turned toward him and handed over the documents he'd requested.

"Allie Parks. Is this your husband's Jeep?"

Her frown pinched her brows so tightly that tiny fissures formed between them. "I'm not married. The car is my father's."

He glanced back to the book on the passenger seat. "Ah, that explains the self-help manual."

Her eyes whipped toward the book. "I don't know what that is."

"Sure, you don't. Just like you didn't know you were speeding. What about crossing the line and almost taking out the Lexus back there?" He turned his head to look down the road. "If you're looking for love, you'll never find it dead."

"I'm not looking for love, and I…" She shook her head in frustration. "I wasn't going twenty miles over the speed limit." Her entire demeanor changed in an instant. The creases lining her forehead disappeared, and the crinkles at the corners of her eyes increased as she smiled. She leaned forward and stared at his name badge. "Officer Rossi?" she asked as if he'd switched names with someone else. "Maybe I was going a wee bit too fast, but surely you can give me a warning and let it be."

He watched as she purred the words and paired them with a coquettish look. He'd seen it all before. Honestly, half the women he pulled over were barely dressed by the time he got to the window as if a glimpse of skin could make a difference. In Aspen, there was a lot of skin to show. Show him a millionaire, and he'd show you a pair of perfectly enhanced breasts. It was as if they didn't have better stuff to spend their money on than silicone or saline.

A glance at Allie proved his theory wrong. His roommates often referred to a woman's chest as her personality. Allie didn't have a big "personality." Hers was as flat as a board with buttons.

He mentally chastised himself for checking out his perp. "I'll be right back. Stay put."

She huffed and let herself fall heavily against the seat.

He walked to the cruiser with the scent of her perfume stuck in his nose. It was something sweet and floral, not roses but maybe jasmine or lavender. Lavender, that was it. He only knew the scent because his mother had burned scented candles nonstop, claiming they had a medicinal quality that could calm a rabid dog. God, he missed his mother.

He ran her driver's license and found no outstanding warrants, but he could see that she wasn't a stranger to speeding. She received three tickets in the last year alone.

He strolled back and found her sitting with her eyes closed. He took a moment to watch her. Red hair. Porcelain skin. Though her eyes were closed, he knew they were the color of newly bloomed clover.

He cleared his throat. She startled, and her eyes popped open as if he'd appeared out of thin air.

"Here you go." He handed back her paperwork.

He could almost see the cogs turning in her head. He waited a long second to see what excuse she'd offer up next. Bathroom emergency that somehow passed while she'd been sitting there? Migraine and in need of rest? Woman's monthly issues? He'd heard them all.

"Listen," she said. "I can't afford another ticket. Aren't there other options?"

He cocked his head and thought about her words. "Are you trying to bribe me?"

She chuckled. "Would that work?"

"Nope. I've heard it all. The last guy I pulled over

told me he had more money than I had tickets. Is that what you're implying?"

He couldn't read her expression because it was one part appalled and one part you-caught-me. "No, I thought that maybe you could be nice, Officer Rossi." She glanced at the clock on her dashboard and groaned. "Look, I'm going to be late."

He nodded to the book. "Have you got a date? Maybe you plan to put one of those recipes to work."

"Geez, I don't have a date. I'm not married, and I'm not looking. Men are a pain in the ass. There isn't time for them, or for this."

Her outburst caught him by surprise. At the mention of men, her throat seemed to tighten.

"Not my business."

"You seem to make it yours." As if a light went on, she brightened and sat up. "Tell you what. I'll forget about your inappropriate questions concerning my single status, and you forget about the ticket."

He laughed. "Nothing inappropriate going on at all. It's my job to get information. All I'm doing is deducing whether you're a risk on the road or not."

"My marital status influences that?" She let out a frustrated growl. "Seriously, is this what my tax dollars pay for? There are real criminals out there, and you're twisting my nipples about a speeding ticket?"

His eyes grew wide. He'd never heard that phrase but imagined it was the equivalent of breaking someone's balls. At the mention of her nipples, his eyes went straight to the pink shirt that hung loosely against her skin, and right there, poking against the material were the culprits.

Dammit, I need to get my head on straight.

"Today, your tax dollars are hard at work to make the streets safer." He scribbled across the pad. "I could cite you for several things. First, there is the speeding violation. You were going twenty miles over the speed limit. Second, there was the false accusation of inappropriate behavior. That could almost be considered an intimidation technique. The only thing you didn't do was offer cash."

"Would it have worked?" She gripped the steering wheel until her knuckles turned white.

"Do you want to find out?" Despite her father having the name Alistair, he didn't figure her for a rich asshole, given that she was driving a Jeep that was the same make and model as his. If she were rich, she'd be driving a Porsche, a Mercedes, or a Beemer, and the first thing out of her mouth would have been how much will it cost me for you to turn and walk away?

He had a real problem with wealthy people getting away with stuff because they bought their way out of it. His parents were dead because of a rich guy speeding down the road in his Ferrari. He tried to use his influence to get out of prison, but he couldn't. Even though Marco made sure the guy did his time, no amount of money would bring his parents back.

"I will lose my license if you ticket me for going twenty over." She let go of the steering wheel and scrubbed her face with her palms. "That has a lot of implications I don't want to imagine."

"Losing your license is not my problem. Killing a family could be yours if you continue to be reckless."

The green of her eyes dimmed as she nodded. "Okay, I was just hoping you'd have a heart and cut me some slack."

"Ms. Parks, my heart died when my parents did because someone was in a hurry to get someplace." He tore off the ticket and handed it to her.

She grabbed the slip of paper and tossed it onto the passenger seat. "You're not very nice."

He crossed his arms. "Your tax dollars don't pay me to be nice. They pay me to be diligent." He gave her a curt nod and walked away. "I'll see you in ten days." Before he reached his cruiser, he heard her last words.

"That sounds about as pleasant as a root canal."

Chapter 3

Allie sent a text to the real estate agent, letting her know she was on her way. She drove one mile under the speed limit the rest of the trip and kept glancing in her rearview mirror to make sure Mr. Tall, Dark, and Sexy didn't follow, waiting for her to break the law again so he could write her another ticket.

Did I just think Tall, Dark, and Sexy? She shook her head as she pulled into the parking lot at Evergreen. "I'm losing my mind, talking to myself, and thinking Officer Anal Retentive was hot."

She opened her bag and set it on the floor to swipe everything strewn across the passenger seat inside. The last thing to land in her bag was the ticket. It wasn't even one she could pay but the kind that required a court date to sort out. Her purse was in complete disarray because of him.

Sexy my ass. He was arrogant and bossy and had those dark chocolate eyes that surely made other women swoon, but not her because men were as useful as a hangnail.

She flung her door open and climbed out of the Jeep. As she took several cleansing breaths, she stared at the building in front of her. The glass and steel structure was likely an eyesore to the community when it was built, but she loved the Art Deco style that stood out among the rustic influences prevalent in the area. It was an older building, but it had good bones and a fabulous zip code.

With her hand on the front door, ready to pull it open, she glimpsed something to her right. Something khaki and pressed with military precision.

The uniform sent a jolt of awareness through her body. It wasn't pleasant, but it wasn't unpleasant either. It was like an electrical buzz that vibrated deep inside.

"I can't believe you followed me." She turned to face Officer Rossi and immediately realized her mistake. Standing before her wasn't the man responsible for her sour mood, but someone different.

"Excuse me?" he said as he reached over her to get the door.

She walked inside and turned to face him. "Nothing, I thought you were someone else. My mistake."

He smiled and walked toward the elevator. "Are you going up?"

The door opened, and she bolted inside. "Yep, top floor."

He pressed twelve and waited for the elevator to close. "Me too."

She glanced at his name tag. Officer Jones was as plain and unremarkable as his name. With his milky complexion and balding head, she found it hard to believe she confused him with the cop whose name she wanted to forget but couldn't. Officer Rossi appeared to be everything Officer Jones was not. She wondered, if she ran into him someplace else, would he have smiled and opened her door like Officer Jones?

When they reached the twelfth floor, he held his hand against the elevator door and waited for her to exit first.

"Are you looking at the Mason place?"

"I'm not sure. I mean, I'm here to see a place, but..." She reached for her phone to look at the unit number before deciding which way to go. There were two doors. The one to her left opened, and she expected to see the agent walk out, but it was another cop. Only this one was a damn giant. Positively Shrek-like, minus the head knobs and green skin.

As he walked by, he smiled at her. "Afternoon." His meaty palm rose to high-five Officer Jones as he moved toward the elevator. "Dibs on the new girl."

Flabbergasted, Allie pivoted and turned toward the door he hadn't come out of. She was about to knock when it opened.

A tall brunette stood in the doorway and smiled. "Glad you could make it. I'm Theresa. Come on in." The realtor stood aside so she could enter.

Allie knew her brows had furrowed by the strain between them. "I'm sorry I was late." She stepped into the entryway and whispered. "I had a run-in with the law."

"I hope it turned out okay because if you take this

place, you'll be living next door to a few officers." She closed the door behind them.

"Aspen is paying its cops way too much if they can afford to live here." She moved down the small hallway that acted as an entry and entered the living room with its wall of windows. The view was spectacular. In the distance, she saw the groomed mountain landscape that, come winter, would be a playground for outdoor enthusiasts who loved to ski and snowboard. She walked to the glass and pressed her forehead to the cool surface. Eyes straining, she squinted to see if she could make out the tower of Luxe in the next town over, but the farthest she could see was the outline of the lake.

"I thought I might see work from here."

"Oh lord, I hope not. A person comes home to get away from work." Theresa turned her back to the view and pointed out the finer points of the living room. "Being on the top floor, you have the benefit of twelve-foot ceilings, whereas the lower units only have ten." She swept her hand out like a game show hostess. "The flooring is a handmade Italian tile. As you can see, the Tuscany beige goes with everything."

At the mention of Italian, a sour taste entered her mouth. *I bet Officer Rossi is Italian.* She didn't know why he continued to enter her thoughts and chalked it up to her irritation and fear that she might lose her license. She should have been nicer. He told her she should improve her disposition by baking something in that book. At that thought, she harrumphed. He didn't know her. She was as sweet as cotton candy, or at least that was what she told everyone. Was it only weeks ago that her brother told her she had a temper as hot as a ghost pepper? Did she?

All she could do was pray that Officer Rossi didn't show up to court.

"Did you hear me?" Theresa asked.

Allie rushed to where Theresa stood in the kitchen. "Sorry, I've got a lot on my mind." As she looked around, she got dizzy from the kaleidoscope of colors. "Was someone murdered here?"

All the tile was blood red. It covered the counters and the backsplash A single inlaid heart above the sink was the only break from the mess. "She must have loved doing dishes."

Theresa chuckled. "The flat used to belong to Mrs. Mason, who believed that all passion started in the kitchen."

"Do I even want to know what that means?"

"Her husband was Fortney Mason, a renowned chef in his day. Red is known to enhance the appetite."

"Wow. It does nothing for mine." She ran her fingers over the four by four tiles. Even the grout was once red but now looked more of a medicinal pink. "This will have to be gutted." With its dark wood cabinets and red counters, she felt like she'd locked herself in a cave—a bloody cave. "With Mr. Mason being a chef, I would have thought he'd have had a larger kitchen."

"He did, but when he passed away, Mavis didn't want to live in the large flat. She divided it into two units."

"She sold it to the overpaid police officers?"

"Something like that." Theresa's heels *ker-plunked*

across the tile as she walked down the hallway to the bedrooms. "You have a master bedroom at the end. It's got an en suite bathroom. The other two rooms are Jack and Jill and share the second full bath. There's a quarter bath off the entryway next to the coat closet."

Allie rarely missed much, but she overlooked that. "It's a shame they divided the property. I'm not sure I want to share a floor with a bunch of cops. I'm fairly quiet. Don't they have a reputation for working hard and playing hard? You know, all-night poker games and stuff."

Theresa shrugged. "I try not to stereotype. You never really know a person until you know a person."

"You're right." Allie thought about all the times people labeled her and felt ashamed that she did the same without much thought.

"It could be good. If they become friends, the next time you have problems with the law, they might be able to help."

"Unlikely. The guy I got a speeding citation from today was as uptight as a nun in a brothel."

Theresa laughed and moved into the master bath, which had a steam shower and jacuzzi tub. The faint scent of roses filled the air, and she imagined the bath filled with bubbles and rose petals.

The flat was in great shape except for the kitchen. What she wanted to know was if the men next door would sell her their half, and then she could convert it back into its original whole-floor dwelling, but she heard her brother's voice in her head. "If you have enough money for both halves, then you can buy one with little negotiation."

"I'd love to make an offer." She considered how much the normal person would pay for a complete overhaul of the kitchen and deducted it from the asking price. "Will the owner take two for it?"

Theresa's eyes got big and buggy. "That's a quarter of a million less than the asking price."

"It will cost at least half that to remodel. The other half is an inconvenience fee."

Theresa pulled her phone from her pocket, tapped in a number, and walked away. While she negotiated the price, Allie moved back into the living room and stood with her back to the windows looking at the space. She could see a camel covered sofa across from the fireplace. In front of the window, she'd put a small table flanked by two overstuffed chairs. It would be a great morning coffee spot or a place to crochet her lap blankets. Rather than use the dining room space as they intended it, she could expand the kitchen and put a large island that could serve as both a prep counter and a dining table. It wasn't like she did a lot of entertaining. If she wanted to entertain, she had an entire resort at her fingertips.

Theresa came back looking pensive. "Michael Mason inherited the place when his mother died. He's not willing to cut the price that much."

"Is he willing to negotiate at all? This isn't the only property for sale in Aspen." It was the only one she'd been interested in, though. For the location and the square footage, it was a reasonable offer. She would have offered his asking price if it was in move-in condition, but that kitchen was a nonstarter. Besides, things were tighter than usual. Rather than use their last property as equity for the new resort, each of the partners ponied up the funds to buy the building and took out a loan for the upgrades.

Before Luxe at Timberline, she could afford whatever she wanted. Hell, if Kevin Costner or Oprah were selling their properties, she could have paid cash, but right now, things were tighter. She had enough to buy this place outright if the owner would be reasonable, but she preferred to put it on a fifteen-year loan.

She needed to leave enough money in an emergency fund to weather several leaner months if Timberline failed. She wasn't used to failing; never had, but she had to prepare for the just in cases.

"He's willing to take two-point-one million if it's a cash deal. You can have the keys the day he gets the cashier's check."

She considered the offer. Cash wasn't what she wanted, but she could do it. She took a walk through the flat once more and stared out the window at the mountains. She wanted this place.

"Deal." She moved into the kitchen and rummaged through her bag to find her checkbook. She pulled the cookbook out and set it on the counter before digging deeper. "I assume he wants a good faith check?"

"Yes, the standard three percent."

Allie filled the check out and tore it from the book at the perforated line. She tossed her checkbook back into her purse and lifted the cookbook to give it a closer look.

"*Recipes for Love*, huh." Theresa pointed at the inlaid heart above the sink. "Maybe you should keep that there; it seems kind of sweet. Maybe it's a sign."

Allie didn't know how the woman knew she was single until she stared down at her ring-less finger. The saying was always a bridesmaid and never a bride, but she hadn't been either one.

"I don't know where it came from; it just showed up." She pushed it toward Theresa. "You can have it."

Theresa jumped back like Allie was offering a lit torch with the flame side forward.

"If I came home with a book called *Recipes for Love*, my husband would question what I'm selling."

Allie tucked it back into her purse. "Call me with the details. I can have my lawyer transfer the funds right away." She walked out, feeling a lot lighter than she had when she entered. She dialed her brother James.

"Hey, Al, what's the news?" She could hear the excitement in his voice, and he wasn't even the one buying a place. James was happy to live in Dani's Timberline cottage. Though he had money, Dani provided them with a place to live. It somewhat equalized their relationship.

"This is your property-owning sister, and I will need your help." She told him about the place and how it was perfect except for the kitchen.

"Get the keys, and I can have it transformed in a week or two with a full crew."

"You're a miracle worker."

"Nah, I'm just your brother, and I love you. Go home and pack."

She hung up and drove back to her father's estate. She strolled into the kitchen and poured herself a glass of wine. Sitting on a stool in front of the island, she pulled out the cookbook. The front cover was worn as if it had passed through the hands of many cooks. She opened it to the preface and read.

Dear Baker,

Everything I learned about love, I learned from baking.

Everything you need to know about love, you'll learn here.

Because you're reading this, it means you've accepted the challenge of choosing one recipe, perfecting it, and passing on the book.

As with everything in life, baking takes effort. Like love, it can't be rushed.

Have you ever wondered why baked goods require certain ingredients?

We add sugar to bring out our inner sweetness.

Salt gives life its flavor.

Flour is a binder like honesty and faithfulness.

Butter is the guilty pleasure in the mix.

Baking soda lifts like a bright smile on a dull day.

Without these, a cake is not a cake, and a pie is not a pie. Without love, a life isn't worth living.

Baking, like love, should be done with passion.

I challenge you to pick one recipe and only one because love shouldn't be hoarded but shared.

Choose the right recipe, and if you can't decide, open the book to a page and let the recipe choose you.

Share the dessert, but not the book. There will be time for that later.

Remember, a perfect cake, or pie, or cookie is like

perfect love. It takes practice, patience, give and take, resourcefulness, perseverance, and often teamwork.

With love,

Adelaide Phelps

"You've got to be kidding me." She sipped her wine and looked through the recipes that had titles like Cherish Me Cheesecake and Crave Me Cupcakes. There was Indulge Your Desire Date Bars along with Friendly Fruitcake. Comfort Me Carrot Cake came next, followed by Slow Burn Blondies.

She laughed. "The last slow burn I felt was when the tip of my curling iron touched my forehead. The damn thing burned all day." She scrolled through the list, which ended with Passion Pillow Cookies. She mentally traced her path today to figure out where someone would have slipped the book into her bag.

She remembered the call she took at the lodge. It was the only time she left her bag unattended.

"Dani, you sneaky little…"

She dialed her number, and Dani picked up right away.

"Allie, your brother told me the good news. Congratulations."

"It's exciting, but that's not why I called. Do you know anything about a recipe book I found in my bag?"

"A book? What book?"

Allie knew right away that Dani was skirting the subject. Her voice always pitched an octave higher when she was uncomfortable. She'd seen it a dozen times since they hired her as the general manager of Luxe.

"Just a book. Something about recipes for love. And since I'm not interested in love, I think I'll toss it."

"No!" Dani yelled.

"Why so passionate about a book you haven't seen?" Inside, she was laughing. Dani was so transparent.

"I'm not … I just…" She exhaled. "Don't give up on love. Wasn't it you who just this afternoon said you would settle for any kind of love?"

"I'm not really the settling type."

"There's someone for everyone. You just haven't met your someone, yet. Maybe try it. What could it hurt?"

"It's a crock. What in the hell is a Slow Burn Blondie or a Passion Pillow Cookie?"

There was an extended moment of silence. "I don't know, but don't make more than one recipe, or you could jinx the magic."

"Mm-hmm. That magic you know nothing about, right?"

"Please, Allie, just give it a try. Follow the rules because I don't want you to jinx my happiness."

"How could I ruin your happiness?"

"Three words. Forever Fudge Cake."

"No way."

Chapter 4

"Man, I'm telling you, she's hot," Terry said.

"Okay, so a hot chick looked at the place. What's the big deal?" In their work environment, they came across beautiful women all the time. Marco had learned a long time ago that the outside wasn't always indicative of what lived inside a person. A rotten apple was still rotten even if you got the skin to shine.

His roommates, Terry Jones and Cameron Tate, liked to believe they were ladies' men, but one looked like the Hulk and the other like a young Mr. Rogers. Cameron worked out far too much, and Terry not enough.

"All he's saying," Cameron added, "was that she's female and pretty, and it's about time we got more variety on this floor."

"We had Mrs. Mason until she passed away." He sure missed the woman who reminded him of what his mother would have been like had she lived long enough to turn gray. Though Mavis had more money than God, she was down to earth, and it wasn't what defined her. She never used it as leverage in any situation.

"I wasn't interested in dating Mrs. Mason," Terry said. "But the redhead ... she's a different story."

"Redhead?" He was sure it was a coincidence, but he had to be certain. "What does she look like?"

Cameron held his hands against his chest. "Not a big personality, but she certainly has a mouthful, and she's not a redhead. I'd say it was on the blond spectrum."

"Not even, she's a redhead," Terry said. "Maybe even a brunette with highlights. She's got the greenest eyes." Terry held a finger to his chin. "Wait, maybe they were blue."

"Nope." Cameron pointed to the velveteen throw pillow that came with the couch. "They were that color, or brown like a good scotch, or melted dark chocolate."

"I'm surprised you two can arrest anyone given your recall skills."

"It's the lighting in that hallway."

"With Mavis gone, I'm sure we can fix that."

Marco had to cut them some slack. Mrs. Mason had sensitive eyes, so the lighting was dim in the hallway. Thinking about Mavis always made his heart equally warm and achy. If not for her, he wouldn't be living in an Aspen penthouse, and neither would his friends. They'd be in some less than swanky apartment in Timberline. A place their salaries could afford.

It was funny how life put him exactly where he needed to be. He was on the corner when Mr. Mason got mugged. The perp pushed Fortney to the ground knocking him out before he stole his wallet. The poor old man hit his head and never regained consciousness. Marco had excellent recall, unlike his friends, and got a good look at the guy. One day he came into the soup kitchen, and that was that. He arrested him on the spot.

Samuel Mayhew was a junkie that stole Mr. Mason's wallet for a fix. The old man had money but never kept it on his person. Fortney Mason lost his life for a five-dollar bill shoved into his front pocket.

"Terry and I are going to Powders for a beer. You want to come?"

Marco shook his head. "I'm at the soup kitchen tonight."

His friends nodded like twin bobbleheads. "All work and no play make Marco a dull boy."

"All play and no work means dozens of people don't eat tonight. Maybe you should come over and help."

Cameron jumped up and pocketed his keys. "Sorry man, I'd love to help, but April is working tonight." He pushed his hands in front of his chest, mimicking cleavage once again. "You know April, the little brunette with the big personality."

Every man had their thing: Cameron was a breast man, Terry liked legs, and Marco looked deeper. He paid attention to a person's heart. A beautiful face or body lost its allure amidst an ugly personality.

"I think your mother took away the teat too soon, and now you're obsessed," Marco said.

He'd met Cameron's mom. She was a big busted, no-nonsense woman. Cameron was a big man, but that didn't stop his five-foot-nothing mother from reaching up and grabbing his ear if he misbehaved.

31

"What would your mother think if she saw you right this second?"

Marco laughed when Cameron snapped his hands to the sides of his head. "Oh lord, I can feel my ears burn already."

"Be glad you have her man. I miss my mom each day." He ambled down the hallway to the master bedroom and took off his uniform. He grabbed a pair of worn jeans from his closet and a soft cotton T-shirt from his drawer. Sitting on top of his dresser was a picture of his parents.

Angelo and Antoinette were second-generation immigrants from Sicily. Their ancestors had taken a ship into Ellis Island in the forties to build a new life for them and their future children.

Living in the United States had been a challenge for his grandparents, but they believed in the American dream. If they worked hard enough, anything was possible. Somehow the family had made it from New York to Colorado, where his father had also been on the police force in Aspen.

He grabbed his keys and went back into the living room, where Cameron and Terry sat watching the start of a baseball game.

"I thought you were out of here?"

Cameron stood and moved toward the door without taking his eyes from the television.

"Let's go, Terry. April and a craft brew are waiting." The Rockies scored a run, and Marco left them cheering. He made his way to the parking lot and climbed behind the wheel of his Jeep to head toward the soup kitchen.

Somehow, he kept it open despite his lack of resources. Sometimes, soup was all he could serve, but those who came for a meal, an ear to listen, or sometimes just a hug didn't ask for much.

By the time he arrived, the sun sat low in the sky, and an orange hue made the horizon look as if it were on fire.

It was a day very much like today that his parents died. He glanced over his shoulder at the intersection where a speeding driver hit them. Had it really been ten years?

Shaking the thought from his mind, he entered the building with a tiny sign above the door that read Soup Kitchen.

"Evening, Marco," Lisa said from behind the counter. She unwrapped yesterday's leftovers. He'd made a large pot of marinara sauce that they'd repurpose for tonight's meal.

Moving behind the counter, he rubbed his hands together. "What are we serving tonight?" The offerings depended on the donations they received. Sometimes they came in the form of food and other times cash.

During the holidays, when people counted their blessings, they often collected more cash, which they used to keep the kitchen open throughout the year. However, much of that money had gone into needed repairs this year, and things were tighter than usual, which meant they were trying to get blood from a stone.

"The butcher brought over some ground beef, and I picked up hoagies from the day-old bakery in Timberline. I thought we'd serve meatball subs and a salad."

"Do we have parmesan cheese?"

She dug into a bag sitting next to her on the counter and pulled out a shiny green can.

"We're good to go." She began dumping the packages of ground beef into the bowl, along with breadcrumbs, eggs, and Italian spices. "Timmy Horton will go nuts tonight. He loves any kind of sandwich." She donned a pair of food service gloves and began mixing.

"He reminds me of me when I was a kid." Marco washed his hands and put on some plastic gloves to help her roll the meat into balls. "I remember my first meal here. I was about five. Mom and Dad were broke, and they brought my sister and me here. They told us it was a new restaurant." He remembered thinking it was odd that they only offered one meal. "That night, they served Salisbury steak. It was before my dad had joined the force. He got laid off from work as a plumber, and things were tough."

Lisa opened the preheated oven and slid the first tray inside. They would cook the meatballs first and then put them in the sauce to soak up the flavor. That way, they didn't have to spoon the fat from the top.

"So, you were kind of raised here?"

"I was. This place feels like home." They worked side by side without saying another word.

"I think that's the first time you told me that."

"I suppose most people don't brag about their soup kitchen days."

In the silence, he thought about his parents. Memories of them were all over this place such as the hand-painted border that had positive affirmations saying, *Today is the first day of the rest of your life.* Or, *there is no such thing as hunger when the heart is full.*

His parents had used the soup kitchen when things were tight, and once everything was going well for them, they gave back. When they found out the kitchen was closing because of a lack of resources, his father used his connections in town to get donations. There was a fine line for using influence. Marco considered it okay to do so if it helped the masses, but not okay if it only helped the person who had power.

Once the meal was ready, they opened the doors.

Marco spied Timmy in line and walked down to get the boy. "It's meatball sandwich day. Being the expert on all things sandwiches, I thought you should go first."

Timmy threw his hand into the air in celebration. "Sandwiches," he yelled. "Woo hoo."

Marco hefted the kid to his shoulders and walked him to the front of the line.

Chapter 5

Allie paced the hallway at the courthouse. The big brick building was intimidating enough, but facing the judge had her knees shaking. Deep inside, she was a rule follower. Well, ... most rules. She didn't believe women couldn't wear white after Labor Day, and she felt like the speed limit was a suggestion, but otherwise, she was a solid citizen.

If luck were on her side, Officer Pain in the Ass wouldn't show up, and they would drop the charges.

She brushed the wrinkles out of her soft-yellow sundress. She wanted to wear her black suit because it acted like a shield for her, but her brother's voice sounded clear in her head as if he stood next to her, telling her to wear something sweet and unassuming.

She picked the yellow sundress because there was an innocence about it, and she hoped the judge would look at her and show mercy.

Now that her knees were knocking, she wished she'd chosen more wisely. Something happened when she pulled on the custom Gucci outfit. It was like she gained strength from the fabric, the color, and the fit. She always referred to it as her Gucci guillotine because it was her go-to for board meetings, terminations, and takeovers, but not tickets.

When she lifted her head, she saw Officer Rossi walking toward her. Her first instinct was to snip at him, but she didn't have a worthy retort. He was right to pull her over. She had been speeding.

Had that really been ten days ago?

Officer Rossi nodded. "Ms. Parks."

"I was hoping you wouldn't show up." She dropped her chin and looked at the ground. All she saw was his perfectly shined shoes and his uniform pants with their crisp creases running the length of his legs. As her chin lifted and her eyes rose to meet his face, she saw that he wasn't as large as she first thought. Sure, he was tall, and there was enough muscle behind that shirt to do damage, but he wasn't a giant like the cop who lived next door.

In any different situation, Officer Rossi might even be considered nice, but today he was the enemy. What was that saying about killing people with kindness?

"I'm sorry you had to take time out of your day to deal with my irresponsibility." She said the words with a smile although they felt bitter in her mouth. No one in their right mind would call her irresponsible. She helped open ten resorts in ten years. She was a self-made woman who graduated magna cum laude at the Wharton School of Business. Even though her mother was reckless and took off when she and James were kids, that didn't mean that they were too. Despite the lack of maternal care, they still turned out okay; no teen pregnancies or drug problems. They hadn't spent time behind bars. And to her knowledge, neither she nor her brother were sexual deviants.

"Just doing my job. It wouldn't serve anyone well if I wrote tickets willy nilly and didn't follow up. I finish what I start."

She heaved a sigh. "Lucky me." She pulled a smile from some internal storage she kept for emergencies and said, "Anyway, I wanted to apologize if I was curt with you. I've been told I can be snippy when I'm under pressure." Her head hung. "I'm so afraid I'll lose my license." Those were truthful words. She hated to depend on others. She'd learned early on that the only person she could truly trust was herself. While she could afford a driver, she loathed the inconvenience of having to count on one.

Officer Rossi frowned. "I get it, but remember when you speed, you're not only taking your life in your hands but others around you who might become collateral damage because of your recklessness." His voice wasn't harpy but sincere.

"You're right. I'll be more self-aware."

"Good. Sometimes the hardest lessons are the best remembered."

The doors to the courtroom opened, and the morning cases filed out. Officer Rossi walked in ahead of her and went straight to the bench.

The judge rose from his seat, and the two men hugged. Not the one-armed bro hug, but a bear hug like a father would give a son.

"Shit, I'm so screwed." She watched the men interact.

At one point, they looked at her, and the judge frowned, then nodded.

Sometimes the hardest lessons are the easiest to remember. He was making sure she learned her lesson well. She sat at the end of a bench and downloaded the Uber app. If the judge took her license today, she wouldn't be able to drive back to work.

The gavel hit the desk, and court was in session.

"I'm Judge Matthews," his booming voice silenced the room. "Those of you who are here to plead not guilty will wait until you're called upon. Those who intend to plead guilty should proceed to the clerk's office and pay your fine."

She didn't have much choice. To plead guilty, would be the same as turning over her license. She considered bringing their corporate lawyer but thought better of it. She wasn't being charged in a murder case; it was a traffic violation.

When she looked around the room, nearly everyone remained. It was funny to see how many people were willing to throw the dice.

She glanced to her left and saw Officer Rossi sitting on the bench, arms crossed, and a frown marring his handsome face. Coming to court had to feel like watching paint dry. She'd be bored to tears if it wasn't for the stories people told.

The woman up now said she'd been in labor. The problem was the kid on her hip was at least six months old.

"When was the little tyke born?" Judge Williams asked.

"Ten days ago, sir." The mother smiled coyly. "He's big for his age."

Another look at the baby showed he was holding his own bottle, sucking away oblivious to his surroundings. "I'll alert the Guinness Book of World Records." His gavel hit the desk. "Pay your fine, and don't waste my time."

Allie laughed out loud. Every eye turned toward her, including Officer Rossi's. She held up her hands like she was asking, "What?"

Judge Matthews called name after name for everything from parking violations to speeding tickets. Generally, the fines and points were reduced by half. Her hopes grew with each new case.

When he called her name, she walked up to the desk set aside for defendants. Across the aisle sat the attorney for the state.

The judge looked at her over his spectacles. "Mrs. Parks?"

"Ms. Parks, your Honor."

He grumbled something. "You seem to live in the fast lane."

She wasn't sure if he was referring to her driving or her lifestyle. Many would think she spent her time on the town, but most nights she was curled up on the sofa crocheting lap blankets. There was a three-foot-high pile of them sitting in the corner that spoke to her lack of social adventure.

She opened her mouth to speak, but he held up his hand to stop her. "It says here that you have a habit of speeding. On June 10, you were driving twenty miles over the limit. How do you plead?"

She could play it two ways. She could cry, and fuss, and make a scene, and hope the judge would show mercy. Or, she could buck up and admit to her crime—almost. She took one last look at Officer Rossi, who stared back with one eyebrow quirked as if to ask, "Yes, what do you have to say for yourself?"

Her hands knotted together in front of her. "You see, Judge Matthews, I'm in a bit of a pickle here. If I plead guilty, I will no doubt lose my license, which doesn't affect you, but it's problematic for me and my job." She took another breath. "As a responsible adult, I'd like to say I'm guilty because there is a good case against me,"—she held up one finger—"however, I don't believe it was actually twenty miles over the speed limit. Perhaps the county should have their radars recalibrated."

"So, is that a not guilty or a guilty plea, Ms. Parks?"

She pursed her lips and moved them left to right and back again. "It's kind of both. Which one will get me a better deal?"

If she negotiated takeovers or property purchases like she did her speeding tickets, she'd be out of business and possibly homeless.

The judge chuckled. It was the first time she'd seen him smile since her arrival. "Tell you what." He looked at Officer Rossi. "Marco approached me before court went into session. He believes your time is better spent doing community service. I don't normally assign hours for traffic violations, but I'm in a generous mood today."

Her heart stalled. She didn't have time to do community service. Her life was Luxe twenty-four-seven. Could she backtrack and plead guilty, pay her fine, and hire a driver? She glanced at her watch and figured if she got out of there within the hour, she could get James to pick up her SUV and plan for next week's transportation.

"You know what? I think I'll just plead guilty."

Judge Matthews narrowed his eyes. "You lost that chance two minutes ago." He scribbled something on the piece of paper in front of him. "You can choose between Habitat for Humanity or the Soup Kitchen. Plus, you will attend traffic school."

"Both?" She looked around. "No one here got both. Why me?"

She was pushing it, but her ghost pepper temper always heated up when she got backed into a corner.

"Why not you? What's it going to be? Habitat or Soup Kitchen?"

She considered her options while the judge tapped his pen on the desk. "Does Habitat for Humanity have a design department?"

Judge Matthews' eyes blinked like he was prepping for a seizure.

"This isn't HGTV court. I can't attest to a 'design department,'" he finger quoted, "but they have piles of bricks to stack and bins of hardware to sort."

"Soup Kitchen, please," she said.

Officer Rossi or Marco, as his buddy the judge called him, groaned. "That should be fun," he said.

"It will certainly be interesting." Judge Matthew hit his desk with the gavel and dismissed her.

She didn't understand what the exchange meant and didn't wait around to ask. She spun toward the door and walked out, happy to be rid of Officer "Pain-in-the-Ass, Smirky-Smile, Beautiful-Brown-Eyes" Marco Rossi

Once in her SUV, she texted Dani.

I'm in hell. Meet me at Powders.

Dani texted back.

Powders? You never go to Powders.

She looked down at her dress.

I'm not dressed for Halfpipe. In fact, I wasn't dressed right for court. I should have worn the Gucci.

Dots danced across the screen.

Oh no! That bad?

She turned the key and listened to her SUV purr to life.

The worst. If you beat me there, order me two dirty martinis with extra olives.

She put the car in gear and headed toward Powders.

How she beat Dani, she couldn't understand. She definitely wasn't speeding, but when she saw her friend was nowhere in sight, she walked straight to the bar and ordered the first of her many future martinis.

When the door opened, and the glow of the sunset painted the room sherbet-colored, she turned around, expecting to find Dani walking toward her, but instead, she saw Marco Rossi. He stopped dead when he realized she was at the bar.

In his worn jeans and snug T-shirt, he approached and ordered a craft brew. He looked down at her just delivered martini and smiled.

"Bad day?"

She let out a growl that tickled her throat. "The worst. I had to face this cocky as hell cop in traffic court. Can you believe he convinced the judge to give me traffic school and community service?" She pulled the paper from her bag. "Thirty hours. Where am I supposed to find thirty hours?"

The bartender slid his beer in front of him and took the ten Marco held out to pay. "Better than the sentence Judge Matthews was about to hand down."

Her mouth dropped open. "What do you mean?"

"Sentences are at his discretion, and he thought maybe weekends in jail might scare you straight." He sipped his beer. "He doesn't take kindly to irresponsible drivers. Ten years ago, a man on his way to a fundraiser killed his best friend."

She watched Marco's jaw stiffen. The vein on his neck pulsed as if the psi was too high and it might explode.

"Oh, wow."

"Oh, wow won't save the kid whose ball rolls into the street when a speeding car can't stop in time. Oh, wow won't save the guy in the ambulance that gets T-boned on its way to the hospital because the woman driving a Hummer runs through the light despite the sirens."

She stared at her martini and felt like one of her olives had lodged in her throat. "Those are awful examples."

He pushed off the bar. "Those are real-life stories."

As he moved away from her to take a seat where he could watch the baseball game, Dani walked inside.

"Who's the hottie," she gave a side glance toward Marco.

"He's no one."

"No one, my ass. I saw you two talking. There's chemistry there."

"You're right, I'm gunpowder, and he's the spark."

Chapter 6

Marco woke to a loud crash. He bolted from his bed and grabbed his .38 from the drawer. Hugging the perimeter, he moved with stealth down the hallway and into the living room.

Terry and Cameron were on shift today, so the noise couldn't have come from them. Logically, it would have been near impossible for someone to break into his place because he was on the top floor, but the sound was foreign, and therefore, required investigation.

Naked as the day he was born, he entered the living room. Finding nothing out of place, he dropped his weapon to his side and laughed. If the gun didn't scare someone, his nakedness might.

"Note to self, pull on some pants next time." As he walked back to his room, another boom sounded from the kitchen. The noise was so loud the glasses shook and rattled in the cabinet.

He marched back into the living room and down the short hallway to the front door. Cracking it open, he peeked out to see several construction workers removing debris from the unit next door.

Feeling confident that the building wasn't crumbling or a thief wasn't lurking in the corner, he walked back into his bedroom to shower and dress.

A half-hour later, wearing his favorite worn jeans and a T-shirt, he made a pot of coffee, grabbed a bowl of Captain Crunch, and sat down at the table.

He stared at the manila folder he'd put there last night. Ignoring the problems wouldn't make them go away. He'd tried that last month, and the damn folder was still around taunting him with its bleak reality. The Soup Kitchen was in trouble—big trouble.

He didn't have many options. He either had to come up with a windfall of cash, or he'd have to close it down, and the second option wasn't one he'd consider. His parents lost their lives because they loved that kitchen. It was his mother's pride and joy. To come from a place of poverty to having the resources to help others was his mother's greatest accomplishment. She might have even liked the building more than she liked her kids.

Shoving the folder away to put it off for another few minutes, he called his sister, Roxanne, who lived in Washington DC. She too had loved the Soup Kitchen. Working there was how she ended up the director for World Food Program USA.

The phone rang twice before she answered.

"Marco," she squealed happily. "How are you?" Roxanne had the temperament of a yellow lab.

He could have talked to her an hour ago, and she would still act like it was the first time he'd paid attention to her in forever. She was one of those people who sparkled, and the day she left Colorado, his life dimmed.

"I'm good. Just missing my little sister." At thirty-four, she was only two years younger, but he liked to remind her that he was much older and wiser. Ever since she sprouted that first gray hair that she succinctly plucked out, she liked being the younger sister all the more. He wouldn't tell her that he hadn't ever seen a gray hair on his head. With the stress of keeping the kitchen open, that might change quickly. "What's up in the land of make-believe?"

He always teased her about living in the nation's capital because nothing there seemed real. There were the lines they fed you, and then the actual truth. It was all smoke and mirrors, kind of like how he ran the kitchen. It was falling apart, but no one on the outside knew, including Roxanne.

"You know, not much has changed since last week. Donations are down, but that seems to happen in the summer months when people are busy doing other stuff. What about you? What's happening at the kitchen?"

"Numbers are down a little since it's warmer. In the colder months, I think people come to thaw out for an hour or so."

"Are you still serving Mom's secret pasta recipe on Sundays?"

"Like clockwork. A person could plan their calendar by Sunday's meal."

"You're not still running the place by yourself, are you?"

"Nope, Lisa is there most nights. Her husband helps

on the weekends. A few of the regulars show up early to pitch in."

The sound from next door continued. It was a persistent rhythmic thunk that jarred his brain with each hit of a hammer.

"What's that racket in the background?"

"Mrs. Mason's son sold that place. The guys say they saw a woman in the hallway, but I don't know if she's the one who bought it."

"Ooh, a woman? Maybe this is providence helping your love life." His sister was always the romantic, but she was single too.

"I'm not looking for a girlfriend. I've got enough on my plate with the Soup Kitchen and my job. What about you?"

She made a *pffft* sound. "You know most men are assholes, and DC men ... well, they are a breed amongst themselves. But women are mostly charming, and you're one of the good guys—a catch, really. Isn't there anyone who interests you?"

Why his mind went to the sassy little redhead from traffic court, he didn't know. She got under his skin in a bad way. As soon as she heard manual labor, she back peddled and offered to pay the fine. Hell, if she'd paid it in the first place, he wouldn't have had to see her again.

"No one at this time."

"Promise me you'll keep an open mind. If the woman next door is single, maybe you two will hit it off."

"Ugh. You know how I feel about wealthy, entitled people."

"You've got to let it go. Not every rich person is an

asshole. There's a mixed bag with everything. Poor people speed too. Middle-class drivers make mistakes."

"True, but that guy tried to buy his way out of vehicular homicide times two." It still burned him up how Trenton Maxwell waved his checkbook around as if all the money in his account would bring back the people he killed. After they sentenced him, Marco tried to sue him, hoping the money would finance the Soup Kitchen for a while, but it turned out, Mr. Maxwell was all flash and no cash.

"Don't punish everyone for one person's mistakes."

"All right, I think this is where I say goodbye."

"Remember what I said—keep things in perspective. You live in that building, and you're far from being rich."

"I live here because while Mrs. Mason was alive, she basically gave me the place. But, according to her will, I have a year to find somewhere new before her son can sell it."

"Maybe Mrs. Mason gave her the place too."

"Bye, Roxy. I love you." He hung up because he wasn't willing to go another ten minutes listening to why he should forgive and forget. As for the place next door, they listed it for over two million dollars. Anyone who bought it was wealthy by any standard.

The thump, thump, thump of a hammer beat on while he dug into the spreadsheets. There was a bullet list of items that needed to be started or completed. Each time he fixed one thing, another fell apart.

His salary on the force wasn't what anyone would consider substantial, but it paid the bills and a little more.

He'd already taken a personal loan to repair the sinking foundation and flood issues.

He tallied the costs three times to make sure he hadn't made a mistake. The numbers didn't lie. He had far more needs than resources. His head ached from staring at the sheets, or maybe it was the pounding that had gone on for hours.

Not willing to listen any longer, he marched out the door and walked to where all the ruckus was happening.

Standing amidst a cloud of dust in the center of the living room was a man in a yellow hard hat. Since he wasn't wielding a hammer, Marco assumed he was in charge.

"Excuse me," he yelled over the din.

The guy whipped around to face him. "Sorry for the dust." He swiped his hand through the air attempting to displace the fog floating around.

"How long is this noise going to continue?" He pinched his temples between his thumb and ring finger of one hand. "It's brain-busting."

"Ah. You must be the neighbor. I'm James." He pointed to the kitchen, which was down to the two-by-fours. "We've got most of the demolition finished. The worst is over. I've got a full crew on this project, so it probably won't take more than a week or two. Since this is my sister's place, and she's impatient, I'm planning on a week tops. If you can put up with us for that long, I promise the rest of your life will be easy. My sis is a workaholic, so she's not home all that often. When she is, she's as quiet as a mouse. I imagine you won't even know she's around."

He wasn't there all that often either, so there was a chance it would be months before they even met. "What's your sister do?"

"She's the chief operating officer at the new Luxe Resorts."

He'd heard the hotel called The Pines had changed ownership, but since it was in Timberline, it was out of his jurisdiction. He didn't get over there much between his full-time job and the kitchen.

"Well, I'll let my roommates know that you're over here. Tell your sister she's got a couple of cops living next door. It's a safe building."

James laughed. "That should thrill her to death."

He left with the impression that it would do just the opposite. Why did so many people dislike the police these days?

Chapter 7

"Has the new pool furniture arrived?" Allie asked while she checked items off the list in her planner.

"It came today, and Bryce is coming in after the pool closes with his crew to change things out." Dani sat at the edge of her desk. "You know you don't have to worry about every detail. That's why you have me, and I have a staff of capable department managers."

Allie dropped her pen and leaned back. "It's a habit." She moved her neck to the left and to the right until it popped. "I'm a control freak. I know it, but..." she blew out a breath, her lips puffing out as she did. "My life fell apart when our mother took off. She left us with our father, who was too busy running his business to raise two kids."

"I'm sorry that happened. I can't imagine not having my parents. They might be judgmental and all up in my business, but they're always there."

"Mom wanted more. Hell, she took half of everything, and it still wasn't enough. Anyway, the reason I'm telling you this is so you understand why I'm so obsessive. Everything about my life was out of sync for years, and managing my world became important to my survival."

"At least you know who you are. Few people are that self-evolved."

"My self-awareness is the product of hundreds of hours of therapy. When a parent abandons you, it's almost worse than them dying because they're still around. The hurt comes from their choice to not choose you."

Dani pushed off the desk and leaned over to hug Allie. "I choose you. If I could trade my sisters in for a newer sleeker model, I'd pick you." She moved around the desk to the door. "I'm out of here. James is cooking dinner and told me not to be late." She held the door-frame and kicked up a heel. "I think our case of body chocolate came in."

Allie tapped her phone, and the screen lit up so she could see the time. "Holy hell, I'm going to be late for my first day of volunteering." She closed her planner, grabbed her bag, and raced past Dani.

"You're wearing that to the volunteer gig?"

She moved toward the elevators with Dani running close behind. "It's a soup kitchen. How hard can it be to ladle stuff into bowls?"

Dani's eyes traveled down to Allie's shoes. "I know, but the Jimmy Choos?"

"I'll be fine."

"You should have brought a change of clothes. I mean ... these are homeless people."

Allie shook her head. "People are people." The

elevator doors opened, and they stepped inside. "I at least thought far enough ahead to bring the beat-up jeep."

"You'll protect the Porsche, but not yourself?"

"If they want the shoes, they can have them. The place isn't in the finest part of town. The shoes are easier and cheaper to replace than tires."

They rode the elevator to the garage.

"People in the best part of town rarely need a free meal," Dani said.

Allie moved toward the black jeep. She pushed the unlock button, and the lights flashed. "Oh, by the way. I made a plate of those cookies."

"What cookies?"

"You know the ones from the cookbook you know nothing about."

"Oh, those cookies." Dani shrugged. "I don't have a clue."

"Right." Allie climbed behind the wheel of the SUV and took off.

She knew better than to speed. How crazy would it have been to get a ticket for speeding to the place she would serve her sentence for speeding? She drove the exact speed limit, not a mile per hour over or under. She turned the corner, and about fifty yards into the final stretch, flashes of red lit up her rearview mirror.

"You've got to be kidding me." She pulled over and waited for the officer to approach. As he got out of his patrol car, she saw it was Officer Rossi. Heat rose to her cheeks, not from embarrassment but from anger. Without a doubt, she wasn't speeding this time.

He walked to her window and tapped on the glass.

Normally, she would have had her license out, but not this time. Her purse wasn't in reach on the passenger side floor. She'd moved it there to make room for the tray of cookies she had baked.

She pressed the button to roll down the window and looked up into his eyes—whiskey brown admonishing eyes.

"Allie Parks, we meet again."

She went to speak, but the agitation she felt closed her throat. She had to swallow several times before she could talk.

"Now, I know your radar is broken. I wasn't speeding."

His lips stretched into a tight line. "Nope, you weren't."

Her jaw dropped. "Then why are you pulling me over?"

"Failure to signal your turn."

"What? Are you serious?" She pointed to the turn signal lever. "I used it." She pushed it up and down repeatedly to make a point.

"Then it's not working, and I'll have to write you a fix-it ticket. Flip it up, and let's see."

She did as he asked while he walked behind her car and returned.

"It's not working. You'll have forty-eight hours to repair it, or you'll receive a fine."

She let go of the steering wheel, and the blood returned to her knuckles. "Give me the damn ticket. I'm already late to the Soup Kitchen. It's my first day to volunteer, and it's your fault I'll be ten minutes late."

"Do you always blame everyone for your failures?"

"Failure?" she said on the exhale. "I'm not accustomed to failing at anything."

"No ticket, just a warning." He scribbled on the back of a card and handed it to her. "Piss poor planning equals piss poor performance. You should have given yourself more time."

She really wanted to fist up and pop him one in his perfectly chiseled jaw, but she didn't have time for a stint in lockup.

"I was at work."

He seemed to take in her clothes. "Fancy duds to be wearing to the Soup Kitchen. Hope you brought a change of clothes."

"I didn't." She rubbed at her eyes. "I..." she frowned. "Okay." She clenched her teeth. "I planned poorly." She looked at the cookies she made sitting on the seat beside her. They were perfect little pockets filled with peanut butter and chocolate. She thought about offering him one, but he didn't deserve it.

"Looks like you took my advice and baked some sweetness into your life. Are you going to share?"

"These are not for you. I made them for whoever is in charge of the Soup Kitchen in hopes that they'll take it easy on me."

He laughed. "I wouldn't bet on it."

She gave him an exaggerated eye roll. "Can I go now? I'm already late, and I don't want them to think I'm a no show."

He pointed up the street. "By all means, go. Don't forget to take care of that taillight."

"You're impossible."

Out of habit, she flicked the turn signal even though it didn't work. Out of self-preservation, she stuck her hand out the window and signaled with her arm. She moved forward, occasionally glancing in her rearview mirror, wondering when she'd see Officer Doesn't Miss a Thing next. Never, she hoped.

She arrived at the Soup Kitchen with her cookies and met a woman named Lisa with eyes as gray as her hair. Odd blue eyes that seemed to look straight through her.

"I brought these cookies to share." She handed them to her and glanced around the room that looked more like a diner than a soup kitchen. She expected industrial tables like they used in school lunchrooms, but there were small dining tables placed throughout the room like a restaurant. Nothing matched, and it added to the charm. On the tops of each table sat a small vase that held a plastic flower. Too bad they'd thrown out that monstrosity of a floral arrangement from the hotel lobby, the kitchen could have repurposed the flowers.

"I'm sorry I'm late. There's this asshole cop who is a thorn in my side. He seems to be everywhere."

Lisa led Allie into the kitchen where a worn but usable stainless-steel prep counter stood in the center. The place appeared to be falling apart with its patched walls and duct-taped pipes, but it was clean.

Lisa's eyes opened wide. "Does he have a name?"

"Oh, I have plenty of them for him, but his given name is Marco Rossi."

She didn't understand why Lisa started laughing, but by the time she calmed down, the woman's cheeks were beet red, and her eyes were wet with tears. "Sorry, thinking about cops is well..." She swung her hand through the air like she was swatting flies. "Doesn't matter." She pointed to a door in the corner. "You can change in the office. Your purse should be fine there too. There's a hook behind the door."

Allie smoothed her hands over her gray pencil skirt and her white silk blouse. "I won't be changing. Just tell me where you want me."

"Can you cook?"

"I have to cook?"

Lisa whistled. "This should be interesting." She filled a bucket with soap and water and tossed in a towel. "Take this into the dining room and wash down the tables. When the boss gets here, he can decide what to do with you."

Allie hung her bag behind the door, took the bucket, and walked toward the door. "The boss? Aren't you in charge?"

Lisa laughed again. "Nope, there's a chain of authority here." She held her palm in the air. "Here's the boss." She lowered it a smidge. "Here's me." Her hand lowered again. "Here are the patrons." She bent over to gesture toward her knee. "This is you."

"I'm that low on the totem pole?"

Lisa lifted her shoulders. "Everyone is here because they want to be. Everyone but you. You're here because you have to be, and that puts you at the bottom."

"Got it." She carried her bucket into the dining room, pulled out the towel, and wrung the water from it until it was damp. As she moved around the tables, the clickety-clack of her heels sounded on the cement floor.

Just as she finished wiping down the last one, the door opened, and in walked Marco wearing a tight gray T-shirt, jeans, and a smug smile.

Chapter 8

The look on her face was priceless when she realized it was him. The bucket dropped from her hands. The impact of it hitting the floor sent a splash of water over the edge, but it didn't tip over.

"I see you made it." He moved forward and stood in front of Allie.

"I think stalking is a crime," she told him.

"Ticket me." He walked past her into the kitchen.

She stomped after him. The staccato pop of her heels sounded like a day at the shooting range.

"What are you doing here?" Allie called after him.

Marco leaned over and kissed Lisa on the cheek and thanked her for filling in until he could get there.

"No worries. I'm happy to help." Lisa pointed to the tray of cookies on the prep table. "By the way, Allie made these for you."

"I did not," She dashed forward and tried to pick up the tray, but he beat her to them, lifting them up, and holding them out of her reach.

He grinned at her. "You made these for me?"

"No," she shook her head. "I baked them for someone else. Someone who is not you. Definitely not you."

Lisa walked to the back door and waved. "See you, kids, later."

They were alone. "I made them for whoever is in charge of the Soup Kitchen in hopes that they'd take it easy on me," he said, elevating his voice and mimicking her words from earlier. "That person would be me." He thrust out his free hand. "Let me have your log-in sheet."

"Can my life get any worse?" She pushed past him, walking into the office. She reached behind the door and got her purse.

"Probably, I learned a long time ago not to borrow trouble."

She returned and pushed the single sheet of paper toward him. "Trouble seems to live in my rearview mirror, and yet, I can't get far enough ahead to avoid you."

When he took the paper, she crossed her arms over her chest and stood there, tapping her foot against the floor.

"Are you going to sign it or what?"

"Eventually." He shoved the page into his back pocket and picked up a cookie. "First, I need to eat one of these treats you made to bribe me." He made a big deal of picking out the best one. "I wonder if this one is the go-easy-on-you-cookie." He plucked a golden-brown treat from the tray. They were all uniform looking and smelled fabulous. He took a bite, but the minute the filling hit his mouth, he froze. The last time he'd eaten anything that tasted this bad was when Roxy baked a pumpkin pie and forgot to add sugar.

Picking up a napkin, he spit what he couldn't swallow into it, and used a clean part to wipe off his tongue.

"These are dreadful."

"How can you say that? Look at them; they're baked to perfection."

"Have you tasted them?"

She let out a growl. "No, I don't eat a lot of sugar. It makes me cranky."

He knew from the strain on his forehead that his brows almost hit his hairline. "This is you not being cranky?"

"You know what? I don't have to justify anything about myself to you. I'm here to work. And since I'm at the bottom of the hierarchy, or food chain, or whatever this is, just tell me what to do."

He tossed the cookie filled napkin into the trash can and walked to the refrigerator.

"Tonight is an easy night. We're having soup and salad. If this were winter, it would be chili and cornbread."

"You have a food schedule? Doesn't that get monotonous?"

He took a massive silver pot from the refrigerator. "Hungry people aren't that picky." He set the pot on the stovetop and turned the handle, but nothing ignited.

A growl-like rumble filled the air. "Can't catch a break."

"Got that right," she said from behind him.

He pulled a box of matches down from the shelf and lit the gas range manually. "You can pull out whatever we have to make a big salad from the fridge."

She moved to the refrigeration unit and yanked the door open. The handle fell to the floor in front of her.

"Holy hell. This place is falling apart."

He rushed over, picked up the handle, and shoved it back into place. "I've got it," he grumbled. "Go wash your hands. I don't want anyone getting sick because we weren't diligent when it comes to food safety."

"You and your safety." She washed her hands in the deep sink against the wall and returned to the prep table to start on the salad. They worked side by side in glorious silence.

When it neared six o'clock, a knock sounded at the back door. "I'll get it. You finish dicing the tomatoes. Help has arrived."

"More help? Is this how you man the kitchen?" The knife dropped to the table with a clank, and she stepped back. "Do you pull people over and ticket them for bogus offenses and then have your judge buddy sentence them to manual labor?"

He wiped his hands on a towel and bent over until his face was inches from hers. He was so close he could smell the lavender on her skin. Was it lotion? Shampoo? Perfume? He moved back to clear his head.

"I've never had anyone serve their community service hours here, and I'd rather not have you. You're a pain in my ass, but Judge Matthews assigned you to the Soup Kitchen. It's almost like I'm being punished for your misdeeds." He walked to the back door and opened it.

When Dean and Stu walked inside, he nodded toward the soup bubbling on the stove. "You guys ladle, and I'll be there in a moment to help." He walked back to where Allie stood.

She picked up the knife and finished dicing the tomato before she filled the bowls with salad. "I saw you talking to him, and you both looked at me; this was a setup, wasn't it?"

"Yes, I talked to him, but I told him that losing your license wouldn't help anyone. I don't know what you do, where you work, or where you live, but navigating life without transportation would be tough, especially in this town where a taxi costs more than a tank of gas. Maybe I was selfish by asking him to take it easy on you. But it was because I didn't want another mouth to feed when you lost your job."

"Unlikely." The disbelief in her voice was more exaggerated than her last eye roll.

Was she talking about losing her job or the truth he told? He didn't have time to worry about it. There would be a line forming outside, and the sooner he could feed people, the sooner he could get home.

"If being here is such a hardship, I can call him and see if he can switch your hours to Habitat for Humanity. Maybe they've got a new delivery of nuts and bolts you could sort." He left her standing there, staring after him while he marched to the front door and opened it to let the masses in.

Timmy ran straight for him like he did every day. Marco lowered himself to his haunches and waited for the impact.

"Is it sandwich day?"

"Not today, buddy. It's soup and salad day."

The boy grimaced. "Aw. I don't like soup. I always spill it on my shirt, and mommy gets mad."

Marco stood and held out his hand for Timmy to take. "Tell you what. If you promise to behave for your mother, I'll take you into the back where we can make you and your little sister a peanut butter and jelly sandwich."

Timmy turned toward his mom, who had baby Blythe bouncing on her hip and Timmy's sister Holly tugging at her other hand. "Is it okay if I go with Mr. Rossi?"

She nodded. The poor woman looked exhausted. She probably was, considering she was a single parent of three. Her husband was in prison in Denver with no chance of parole for five years. Susan Horton had been seven months pregnant with Blythe when Dillon attempted to rob a gas station. She survived on social programs and the odd jobs she could pick up here and there. They took all of their evening meals at the Soup Kitchen.

"Grab your sister, and let's go."

With a child holding onto each hand, he led them into the kitchen while the line filtered into the dining room.

He found Allie wiping down the prep table. "Can you grab a loaf of bread and the jar of peanut butter from the shelf?" He pointed to the almost empty metal supply rack. "I'll see if we have some jelly left."

She looked at the two little ones and smiled. "Discerning guests tonight?"

"VIPs. We aim to please."

She came back with the bread and peanut butter and squatted in front of the kids. She looked down at the rip in the fabric moving up her thigh. "Dang it." She stood and attempted to yank the ends together, but it was no use. She couldn't fix the tear by tugging.

"Told you," he said. "Poor planning."

She ignored him and set out four pieces of bread and opened the jar of peanut butter. "Do you like it thick or thin?" While she waited for the kids' answers, she moved the tray of cookies to the edge. "If they're peanut butter lovers, they'll appreciate my cookies."

"We'll see," Marco said.

"Want a cookie?" she asked.

Both kids swiped one from the plate and took a bite. In unison, they spit it onto the floor. "Yuck." Timmy wiped his mouth with the palm of his hand. Holly stood there with her tongue hanging out as if waiting for someone to clean it off.

Marco swept her up and took her to the sink, where she sipped water from the faucet and spit until the taste disappeared.

Allie stared at the cookies. "I don't know what you guys are complaining about. It's basically a sugar cookie stuffed with peanut butter and chocolate. I used the good peanut butter too. It's organic."

"It's disbusting," Timmy said.

"You mean disgusting," Marco corrected.

"You guys are crazy." She swiped a cookie from the

tray. "I'll prove that these are delicious." She picked one up and took a bite.

Marco watched her face turn from cocky and confident to horrified.

She rushed to the trash can and spit it out, then marched back to the prep table, picked up the tray, and dumped the rest of the cookies into the bin.

"Was that thick or thin?" she asked the kids when she returned to sandwich making.

With sandwiches in hand, Marco led Timmy and Holly into the dining room while Allie went to the office to find a solution to her splitting seam problem.

He was seeing a different side of her. Sure, she was still snarky and had a smart mouth, but she also proved she could be kindhearted and patient with everyone but him. Then there was the skirt mishap. Most women would lose their minds if their clothes got torn, but not Allie. She was a puzzle he hadn't figured out yet.

She walked into the dining room with a tear from her knee to her hip, and boy did those legs look good in a skirt held together by safety pins. She'd drive half the men insane with the little glimpses of skin that rose up her thigh.

"What should I do?"

"You could refill bowls and water glasses."

"Okay, then what?" She looked around. "This is like a restaurant. It's not ... not what I expected it to be."

"This is home to a lot of people. I try to make people feel like they belong."

He watched as she looked up to read the border that wrapped around the room.

"Never let the things you want make you forget the things you have," she recited. "I like that. Did you put that up there?"

He shook his head. "No, my mother did."

Allie smiled. It was a beautiful sight when her eyes lit up like sparkling emeralds.

"She must be an inspiration to everyone here."

"She was."

Her smile fell. "Oh. I'm sorry."

"Me too." He set his hand on her shoulder. "Meet the people you serve. One of the biggest complaints from those who have little means is that no one sees them. People look the other way and pretend they don't exist."

"That's awful." She scrunched her nose and leaned in. "Are you sure it's not because homeless people usually smell bad?" she whispered.

He shook his head. "I have three rules for the Soup Kitchen. Number one is everyone gets along. Two is there is no drama allowed, and three is everyone has to bathe. The boxing gym down the street sets aside a shower stall for those who need it."

She stepped back and looked up at him with something that looked akin to confusion. "You're not who I thought you were."

"Who is that?"

"A total asshole."

"You never know, I might fulfill your expectations by the end of the night."

He took an empty seat at a nearby table and enjoyed a bowl of soup with some guys while they talked about baseball.

All the while, he watched Allie. It surprised him to find her warm and inviting. She talked with Susan Horton. He imagined they didn't have much in common, but it was fun to see the mother of three laugh and enjoy female companionship. Allie played with Timmy and Holly and cradled little Blythe to her chest while Susan ate. Over the following hour, the crowd trickled to the few who usually stayed late to help clean up.

Allie didn't say a word when he sent her to tidy and restock the bathrooms. She did the least pleasant job in the place without complaint.

As she grabbed her purse and readied to leave, he realized that she was nothing like he thought, either. Driving her daddy's jeep didn't make her a spoiled rich girl. It just made her a girl who drove her father's car. Maybe his sister was right. Maybe he was cynical. He was and needed to change that.

She stood in front of him and tilted her head back to see him. "So, I'll be back tomorrow and the next day, but probably not Friday. I've got some things to take care of."

"A hot date?" He imagined someone who looked like Allie had a lot of dates. She was petite and pretty, but she was also a spitfire. She reminded him of one of those little dogs that thought they were ferocious. Why was it, the smallest animal always had the biggest attitude?

"Why are you so obsessed with my dating life? Are you interested, Officer Rossi?"

"Not in a million years, sweetheart. Just curious." Why was he? Allie Parks was annoying. She was like an itch he couldn't reach. An irritating fly he couldn't swat away. She entered his life like a bad rash. "The sooner you complete your hours the better."

"That's the plan. Once I complete my time, I'll be out of your life for good."

Her statement stung a little. He was a good guy, and like his sister said, by all standards, quite a catch. "You'll miss me when you're gone. You could do worse than me."

"No way. I've sworn off men for a lifetime."

"Or scared them off with your attitude."

She shrugged. "Looks like my RBF is working."

He lifted his brows. "RBF?"

"You know, resting bitch face. I've been perfecting it since the last idiot I dated. I'd say it's as effective as a sign that says I have syphilis."

His head snapped back. "Do you?"

"No, but I have little need for men either."

"Noted, and since I wasn't offering, it's a moot point."

"Anyway, back to my schedule, I will be here on Saturday. Might as well get it over and done with. You are open on Saturday, right?"

"People eat on Saturday too."

"Right, well, I should have it all under control by then."

"Under control? Is everything all right?" He probably shouldn't have asked. He shouldn't have cared, but he did.

She waved him off. "Yes, it's all good. I'm moving out of my dad's, and into another place."

"Finally clipping the parental apron strings? Daddy cut you off?" He hated himself for assuming, but Alistair Parks lived in one of the priciest neighborhoods in Aspen.

She fisted her hands on her hips. "What is wrong with you? My father doesn't spoil me. He lost that ability when my mother left twenty-five years ago and took everything with her. The only reason he's got that house is because she hated the cold." Her cheeks turned red. "Not that it's any of your business."

He'd misjudged her again. "I'm sorry. I..." he shook his head. "Sometimes, being here and seeing how desperate these people are, clouds my senses. There's such a gap between the haves and the have nots."

"Well, don't punish me for other's mistakes. I try to help everyone. I try to give more than I take." She looked around the kitchen, frowned, and shook her head. "What else can I do?"

Feeling shitty for judging her, he said, "Nothing, you already helped. You showed up, and that's more than most people do."

Her chin fell. "I was court-ordered."

He reached forward and thumbed up her chin. "Yes, you were, but you weren't court-ordered to be nice. That came from your heart."

She walked to the door. "Don't pull me over anymore. My heart can't take it."

"Stop breaking the law and get that light fixed." His voice didn't hold his usual stern, no-nonsense clip. It had a hint of a tease in it.

Her tense shoulders eased as if they'd come to some kind of truce. "Are you always so bossy and hard to deal with?"

"No, sometimes I'm worse."

Chapter 9

Allie brought a change of clothes to work along with a tray of store-bought cookies that sat on the passenger side of her car.

She parked next to Dani, who was exiting her SUV.

With her jeans, T-shirt, and Keds tucked under her arm, she exited and rounded the Jeep.

"Hey, why are you here so early?" Allie always beat everyone to work by an hour. She liked that quiet time before the storm. Normally, she'd sit at her desk, sip her coffee, and review her to-do list. Staying organized was the only way she could juggle so many balls and not have them fall.

Dani smiled like a kid ready to see Santa Claus. "They finished the suites, and I can't wait to see the new tile and slipper tubs."

"Let's grab a coffee at Pikes Perk, and I'll come with you to look." Allie shoved her clothes into her bag and headed out of the garage to the sidewalk. They moved side by side to the coffee shop across the street.

"One sugar-free, caffeine-free, fat-free latte," she told the cashier. After a glance at Dani, she added, "One cup of sugar with a splash of coffee."

They leaned against the counter and waited.

"How did it go last night?" Dani gathered two napkins and a stir stick.

Allie didn't know how she sucked down that much sugar and didn't end up in a coma.

"It was okay." She quickly replayed the evening in her mind. "I mostly wiped tables and prepped salads." She was about to change the subject back to the suites when she realized Dani didn't have all the details. "Oh. My. God. I almost forgot. You know the cop who pulled me over?"

"Not personally, but go on."

"He runs the Soup Kitchen, and I can't figure out if he set me up or if it's simply bad luck for both of us."

"Why bad luck for him? You're free labor."

"Because he has to deal with my attitude."

"But you brought him the cookies. That should have helped."

"Holy hell, the cookies are a whole different matter. They looked terrific, but they tasted like..."

"Monkey butt?"

She shook her head. "Worse, they were peanut butter filled ape ass."

An older woman looked up from her paper and scowled. "In my day, we didn't cuss in public. It's not becoming for a lady."

It had been a long time since anyone had chastised

her, and she kind of liked it. This woman, who didn't know her, said what her own mother wasn't around to say: *Potty mouths aren't pretty.*

"I apologize."

She gathered her empty cup and crumpled her napkin then rose to shuffle toward the trash can. "In my day we said, 'Oh piddle diddle' or 'fiddlesticks' or 'gull durnit.' Where are people learning their manners these days?" She didn't wait for an answer but frowned and lumbered away.

When Allie turned back to Dani, she was furiously typing on her phone.

"What are you doing?"

"I'm sending Trish more words for her arsenal of non-cussing foul language. Fudge monkey loses its effectiveness when it's said all the time."

"Order up for Allie," the barista called.

"Anyway, back to the cookies. They were shi … cruddy. Even the kids spit them out."

With coffees in hand, they took off toward Luxe. "You must have done something wrong."

"No, I was pedantic with the recipe."

"What did you make?"

"Passion Pillow Cookies." They crossed the street and rounded the police cruiser parked at the curb. Each time she saw anything to do with law enforcement, she thought about Marco and his scowl, and thick hair, and muscled chest. Not that she was looking, but when he walked into the Soup Kitchen wearing a cotton shirt that hugged his torso, it was hard not to notice.

"What's a pillow cookie?"

"It's a disaster. There's no passion in that recipe. It's basically a sugar cookie you fill and bake. It comes out tasting rancid."

They walked through the front doors into the lobby.

"What did you fill it with?"

"I told you already. Peanut butter. Remember, peanut filled ape bottom?" She marched ahead until she reached the flower centerpiece. Beyond it stood none other than Officer Rossi. He stood in front of the counter, talking to one of the front desk clerks. "Get down." She squatted behind the table and pulled Dani beside her. "That's him."

Dani lifted to look. "That's the guy from the bar." She lifted again. "He's a police officer?" She turned to face Allie. "Oh my God, he's *the* police officer."

Dani pinched her side, making her yelp.

"He's the stupid piddle poop that's responsible for my miserable life."

"Isn't that dramatic?" Dani peeked up again. "He's gone."

Someone behind them cleared their throat and dread washed over Allie.

"Did you lose something, ladies?"

Allie wished the marble floor would open up so she could sink into it and disappear forever.

Dani hopped up. "Hi, I'm Dani, and I think you know Allie."

Since she couldn't crawl away without making a scene, she stood. "Hello, Officer Rossi."

"Allie?" He quirked a brow that made him look sexier than his uniform. Who knew she liked a man in uniform? She generally dated men who wore suits, but wasn't that the uniform for executives?

She pulled back her shoulders and stood as tall as her heels would allow. "Have I broken some law, and now you're here to arrest me or ticket me?" She hoisted her purse strap to her shoulder and thrust out her hands. "I'll go quietly."

He chuckled. "That might be a first."

"So, you do know her." Dani smiled and stepped back as if she were watching a live performance of her favorite show.

He rubbed his chin, which had a shadow of whiskers already darkening his skin.

She wasn't sure if it made him look more desirable or dangerous. Maybe both.

"We are acquainted, but I'm not here for you. An employee was in an accident this morning, and I was following up."

Dani's face fell. "Were they hurt?" She glanced at Meg, who seemed to be fine.

"No, just a fender bender." He looked around the lobby as if seeing it for the first time, then stared at Allie. "Do you work here?"

Dani choked. "Work here? She's the—"

"Human resources. I work in the HR department."

Dani gave her a what-the-hell look.

"While I'd love to stay and chat, Officer Rossi, we have a meeting to get to."

"We do?" Dani asked.

She implored her with a look that she hoped said, "play along," but feared it said, "I'm getting ready to pee my pants."

"Yes, that meeting with your boss. You know, the one who will make your life miserable if you don't get going?"

"Oh ... that boss." She shook her head, but she didn't drop the big grin on her face. "That one is a piece of work. She's like a drill sergeant or a mean headmistress at a girls' school. A rabid dog, really." She held up her cup of coffee. "Especially when she doesn't get what she wants."

Allie cocked her head. "She's not that bad."

Officer Rossi cleared his throat. "Well, I'll leave you to face your tyrant."

He turned and walked away, but as soon as he was out of earshot, Allie asked, "Am I that bad?"

Dani busted out laughing. "No, but you should have seen your face." They walked to the elevator and rode it to the 13th floor. "Why didn't you want him to know you owned the place?"

She chewed the inside of her cheek while she contemplated the question. "I don't know. He seems to have a problem with wealthy people. He knows I have money, he's pretty much deduced that from my father's address and my clothes, but he doesn't have to know how much money I have."

"Why does it matter?"

She let out a huff. "Because as much as I dislike the man, I want him to see me as a person first."

"You saw how well that worked out for your brother?"

"It turned out fine in the end. Besides, I'm not dating Officer Rossi."

Dani chuckled. "Nope, not yet."

Chapter 10

She showed up wearing jeans and a smile. If he didn't know that she was court-ordered to work at the Soup Kitchen, he could almost believe she liked it.

From across the room, he watched her play with Timmy and Holly for a few minutes before she offered them a cookie.

They stared at it. Holly backed away and shook her head, but Timmy was brave and grabbed the sun-shaped, orange sprinkled cookie, and took a bite.

"Trying to poison the kids again?" he said, as he made his way to where she knelt before them.

"I can't believe you think I'd poison these beautiful babies." She popped up on her Keds, and he saw for the first time how tiny she was. Even in the courtroom, she'd worn a kind of wedged sandal that gave her a few inches. "Now, you, on the other hand..."

He plucked a cookie from the tray and handed it to Holly, who was still skeptical but gave in when her brother took a second one.

"Sun cookies?"

Allie smiled. "Yep, just spreading my sunshine around. Don't you worry though, I plan on perfecting that recipe and bringing you another batch."

"Thanks for the warning." He stood beside her and breathed in her lavender scent. "Is it your shampoo? Perfume? Lotion?" He leaned down to catch a closer whiff. "Lavender, right?"

She lifted her chin and beamed. "Yes, it's all the above. How did you know?"

He shrugged. "My mother liked to burn candles in the house."

"She was a smart woman. I'm sorry for your loss."

He wanted to dislike her, but he couldn't, sure she was reckless, and he was certain she was manipulative given his first run-in with her, but there was a softer side —a side that he figured she didn't show many people. He saw it each time she interacted with Timmy and Holly.

"It's been a long time, but you don't really get over losing your parents."

"You can say that again." She stiffened as if she'd made a mistake by letting her guard down. "Anyway, it's a calming scent, and I'm high-strung, so I find it helps me relax."

His hand was halfway to her shoulder to let her know she could trust him when Susan came over with a fussy baby Blythe.

"Would you mind holding her for a second so I can grab a plate of food and a minute of rest?" Her southern twang got stronger with each word. "I'm plum tuckered out, and that bowl of stew is calling my name." She looked between Allie and him.

Allie beat him to the baby, who was a plump thing with rolls on her thighs. There was no concern that Blythe wasn't cared for.

"Look at you," Allie cooed as she cradled the baby in her arms. "Give me a smile." She tapped her little nose and made a world of sounds that scored her a laugh.

"She looks good in your arms. I haven't asked, but do you have children?"

She turned to him and frowned. "Officer Rossi, are you obsessed with my status? First, you hound me to find out if I'm single, and now you want to know if I've got kids. I told you I'm not married."

He chuckled. Riled up Allie was cute too.

"Ms. Parks, both of us know that marriage isn't a prerequisite to having children. Look around you." He glanced around the room that had as many kids as adults. "Half of them come here for a meal because they are single parents, single-income families. I was just trying to be"—he lifted his shoulders—"nice."

Her nose wrinkled, and she hugged Blythe to her chest. "I'm sorry. I just ... don't like sharing a lot about myself."

"Fair enough." He took a step forward, and she reached out to pull him back.

"To answer your question, no, I don't have children. I'm thirty-two, and that ship is quickly sailing past me."

It surprised him that she thought that. "Not true, there was a seventy-year-old woman in India who gave birth recently."

"Just shoot me. I know it can be done, but honestly, if I ever have a baby, I kind of want a husband beforehand. Finding a good man hasn't been all that easy for me. My job requires a lot—it takes up a lot of time."

He almost forgot about finding her crouched behind the table in the lobby.

"Speaking of your job, were you hiding from me?"

She blushed. Her cheeks turned almost as red as her hair.

"Well, ... yes. You're not what I'd call a good luck charm. Each time I see you, something bad happens."

His jaw dropped open. "What do you mean? I'm bad luck for you?"

She looked to the ceiling as if the words were hanging there, and she could pluck them free.

"You want a list?"

Did I? "I'd love a list. I'm a list kind of guy."

Her green eyes sparkled. "Something we have in common. Imagine that. I'm all about the lists. So, here goes:

You pulled me over.

You gave me a ticket.

You made me late.

I had to take time off for court.

I got sentenced to manual labor.

I'm spending my weekend in traffic school.

I had to fix the blinker on the Jeep.

I ruined my favorite skirt.

I need a manicure from the bleach water I used to wipe the tables.

Should I go on?"

"There's more?"

Blythe fussed, and she switched positions, propping the baby on her hip to give her a little bounce. Each time she moved, her arm caressed his, sending a jolt of awareness through him.

"You have no idea, but I'll leave it at that."

He smiled and stepped back. "Misery looks good on you, Allie. Especially when you smile, it must be awful to look so happy. The minute you get here, you can let the rest of the stuff go. I'd say lavender isn't your scent at all. It's soup kitchen."

"When was your last eye exam, Officer Rossi? I think your vision is skewed."

"It's Marco, and I see perfectly. You like it here, and I think you may like me more than you want to admit."

He waited to see if she'd deny it, but she didn't. She smiled coyly and said, "That would make your day, wouldn't it?"

Although he wouldn't admit it, it would. "Now who's dreaming?"

THE NEXT DAY, Allie was late.

"I'm so sorry. Things at work got busy. There was a small fire in the boathouse I had to look into. The produce delivery was late—again. It was a total shit show from the minute I arrived at Pikes Perk this morning, and their frother didn't work. No coffee makes Allie an unhappy camper."

She sucked in a deep breath and let it out. He could almost hear her internal voice count to ten as she exhaled.

"Why would a human resource employee have to deal with a fire and a produce order?"

She stilled, and her eyes grew wide. "Well, when an employee starts the fire, it's an HR issue, and when the chef threatens to skin the delivery driver alive, it becomes my problem too."

"Grumpy much?"

"Just let it go. I had a busy day, and I'm tired."

He pulled six roasted chickens from the big oven. "All I'm saying is it seems to me like your company is taking advantage of you. You'd be less tired if you weren't putting out everyone else's fires."

"Haha, pun intended?"

"No, but I imagine the COO, or the CEO, or the hotel manager could do those things."

With her hands fisted on her hips, she stood at the prep table and glared at him.

"What do you know?"

"I know the chickens are done, and those green beans in front of you need cleaning, trimming, and steaming. I also know that people will take advantage of you if you let them." He turned off the oven and stirred the pot of mashed potatoes. They were the boxed kind, but they were cheap, and no one complained.

"You're right, but in this case you're wrong. I've been taken advantage of plenty of times, but it's by selfish men. Take this little gig, for instance. How interesting that I end up in *your* soup kitchen doing *your* dirty work."

He nearly dropped a chicken. "Are you still going on

about that? I don't know why he put you here. I think it was to drive me nuts. Payback for the last time I emptied his pockets playing poker."

She tore the ends of the beans off and tossed those bits in the nearby trash can. "Gaming is illegal in the state without a license."

He took the big butcher knife and cut up the chickens. "Well, Officer Parks, you're wrong. As long as I do not hold a game for profit, it's legal."

She stared at him like he'd spoken in tongues. "You just said you cleaned out his pockets. I'd call that a profit."

"No one charged anyone to take part in the game. There was no buy-in, and it was a bona fide social gathering, so it's called social gambling and falls perfectly within the limits of the law." He swung the butcher knife down to divide the breast in half. "Do you gamble?"

"No, I'm too smart and work too hard for what I make to piss it away in a game of cards."

He narrowed his eyes. "You drive your dad's Jeep and live in his mansion in the woods. Why are you working when you probably still get an allowance?" Where that came from, he wasn't sure. Her comment about being too smart implied he was dumb, and that stung.

She twisted the beans and snapped them in half. Her pretty mouth contorted until her lips pinched. "You know what? I was wrong. You are an asshole."

She gathered the beans and tossed them into the bowl, then shoved them into his chest. "Steam them yourself. And for your information, I stopped getting an allowance the day my mother abandoned me. I was six. I may live in an awesome zip code, but I've earned every dollar in my account." She stomped her foot and glared at him. "You can hate me all you want because of what you see on the outside, but you don't know me. You have no idea what's in my heart and soul." She turned and stomped away.

He watched her disappear into the dining room. How had everything gone so wrong?

He looked down at the green beans. If she'd held them for five more minutes, they would have been cooked through by the heat of her fiery temper.

She was right. He was an asshole.

The rest of the night, they moved around each other like oil and water, never really mixing just swirling in the same container.

When she gathered her things and headed for the door, he said, "Allie, I don't know what happened tonight, but I'm sorry. I guess I am an asshole."

She tugged her purse onto her shoulder. "At least we agree on something." She pushed the handle and disappeared out the back door.

Chapter 11

James led a blindfolded Allie into the penthouse. He was a day late with delivery, but taking Friday off gave her time to pack her stuff.

The flat smelled like freshly cut pine cleaner. She imagined it would smell like baked goods in a few days or, her favorite pasta sauce that she simmered on the stovetop for hours.

"Are you ready?" James asked.

"I've been ready since I bought the place."

She would have rolled her eyes, but it would have been anticlimactic given that he covered them.

He moved her forward and tugged off the kitchen towel he'd tied around her head. In front of her was a masterpiece. Gone was the red tile and old appliances, and in their place was perfection. Off-white antiqued cabinets lined the walls. A side-by-side refrigerator and freezer hid behind corresponding panels. The floors matched so flawlessly that there was no indication that the kitchen floor was a later edition.

"How did you find the exact tile?"

James smirked. "I have connections."

She walked forward and ran her hand over the smooth granite with veins of gold and silver.

"It's perfect." This was the first house Allie had purchased. Her other homes were rentals because up until now, her life was nomadic, living near the next property they converted. But with Luxe being the last, or at least the last for now, it was time to lay down some roots, and Aspen had always felt like home. It was where their father took them to acclimate to the new world order once their mother had left. They'd licked their wounds and grown stronger. Somehow, she always felt like a sapling that sprouted above the alpine tree line. She was tiny but mighty, and the bumps along the road only made her more resilient.

"I'm glad you like it." He pulled a frame from a shelf in the cupboard. "I know you hated the red tile. It was awful, but I had to save this piece because it seemed important, like somehow, love had been the cornerstone of the kitchen." He handed over the frame, which had the single tile with the white inlaid heart.

She stared at it. Why a white heart? Was it because it was pure? Or maybe it was because it stood out against the crimson tile.

"Thank you." She held it to her chest and willed the tears that pooled in her eyes away. "You gave your heart to me."

"I saved it because I think love could live here again if you opened yours."

She set the picture on the counter. "My heart is fine the way it is."

James walked around her and opened the cabinets to show the built-in spice racks and drawers for pots and pans.

"I met your neighbor the day we started, and he seems like a nice guy. I think you'll like him."

"The balding cop or the hulk?"

He cocked his head to the side. "Umm, that doesn't sound like him. He's about this tall," James raised his hand a few inches above his head. "He's dark-haired, and you know, he's a guy."

She laughed. If it were a woman describing anyone, she'd have the dirty details down to the length of his eyelashes. "Glad he seems nice. I'd hate to have an asshole for a neighbor." She immediately thought about her closing conversation with Marco the other day when she told him he was exactly who she thought he was—an asshole. What had he said? *Sometimes I'm worse.* Or, was that when she said he was bossy?

"I was just thinking."

She reached up and pinched his lips closed. "Don't say it." She dropped her hand. "Just because you're in love doesn't mean I need to be."

"Hear me out." He stepped back. "Not all men are after your money. The way I see it, he lives here in a swanky penthouse. That has to say something."

"It says he's got good taste in property, but that's about it. He also has two cops for roommates, but right now, I'm not a fan of law enforcement."

James leaned against the counter. "That's right. You've got those community service hours. How's that going?"

She moved the framed heart around her kitchen until she found the perfect place for it next to the stove.

"It went better than I expected. I sacrificed a perfectly good skirt, but it was okay. I never stopped to think about soup kitchens. I always assumed they were there to help the homeless."

"I'm sure that's true."

"The word homeless fills my imagination with visions of dirty alcoholics sitting on the street corner, begging for change, but it was more than that. There are mothers and children and good honest people that need a hot meal and a place where they feel like they belong."

"No smelly drunks?"

"The guy who runs the place, which is the same guy who ticketed me, has three rules, and one is they have to be clean to enter."

"Does he hose them off at the door?"

"The gym down the street lets them use a shower stall. The point I'm trying to make is the guy treats them all the same. He has expectations, and they somehow rise to them."

"Is there any way we can help?"

"I'll ask. I've got to work off more hours tonight. The place is a disaster. A big beautiful disaster."

The buzzer rang, and Allie rushed to the intercom to answer. "Hello?"

"Furniture delivery for Allie Parks."

She buzzed them in. "Top floor. Unit to the right."

James shook his head. "You already arranged for furniture?"

"I'm not staying one more night in that big house."

"I get it. I'm out of here."

She gave him a pout. "Can you do me one last favor and bring up the boxes from my car? It's just clothes and stuff."

He frowned. "I knew I'd get suckered into more."

"If you want to do more, you can stay and help arrange the furniture."

"Nope, I know how you are. You allow yourself three tries for every piece, and you use them all. I'll do the boxes, but then I'm gone. My guys are refurbing the outdoor recreation department because the fire yesterday moved it to the top of the list."

She walked him to the door. As she opened it, her sofa arrived.

The rest of the day was filled with delivery after delivery until the empty apartment was full of furniture. Little by little, it felt like home.

Exhausted, she sat on the stool at the counter and opened the cookbook her brother had found on the front seat. Because he set it in a place she couldn't ignore, she figured he was in cahoots with Dani.

She scrolled through the index of goodies. The cookies were obviously a fail. Seeing three people feel the need to wipe off their tongues was both alarming and entertaining. That recipe wasn't one that would bring her love. It might bring her a lawsuit if she inadvertently poisoned someone.

She scrolled down the list to see if anything else sounded interesting, but her eyes kept going to Passion Pillow Cookies, and her mind kept going back to Dani and her warning to only choose one recipe. Was there really a rule about the number of sweets she could bake?

Turning to the preface, she read it again until she came to the line, *I challenge you to pick one recipe and only one because love shouldn't be hoarded but shared.*

"Well, dammit." She never gave superstition much thought, but seeing how in love her brother and Dani were and remembering that Dani begged her not to jinx her happiness, she considered the consequences of ignoring the author's directions.

Erring on the side of caution, she would stick to the cookies. The last time she baked them, everything turned out okay except the filling. She went back to the recipe and reread it. At the bottom, in tiny little letters, it said, "In case of failure turn the page."

Failure?

She closed the book. "I'm no quitter." She tapped the screen of her phone and saw she only had fifteen minutes before she needed to leave the house for another day of court-ordered torture. Funny how she'd labeled it that, but deep inside, she was looking forward to seeing Susan, Timmy, Holly, and Blythe. And if she were honest with herself, she didn't mind seeing Marco again. While he was a bear to be around, he was nice to look at.

Dressed in jeans, a slouchy tunic, and a pair of Keds, she walked out of her place. She turned to find Marco coming out of her neighbor's door.

The world moved in slow motion as his head cocked to the side.

She froze in place with her key still in the lock. The only words that came to mind were, "You've got to be kidding me."

Chapter 12

"You can't be serious." He couldn't believe that Allie was his new neighbor. "Please tell me you're visiting a friend."

"You can't be the neighbor my brother claimed was nice."

He held out his arms. "I'm nice. What's not nice about me?"

"Do you want the list again?"

"No, but I want the truth. Your brother said his sister was the COO of Luxe. You lied to me."

She moved toward the elevator. "I did not."

"Bullshit." He marched after her. "You said you worked in human resources. That's not the same as being the chief operating officer. What's your game?"

The door opened, and she walked inside, hitting the first-floor button repeatedly.

"I don't have a game. What's your problem?"

Heat rushed to his face. "You are." No single person riled him up as effectively and efficiently as Allie Parks.

She made the vein on his forehead pulse almost painfully.

When the elevator door opened on the first floor, she brushed past him. "You've got me for another few weeks, and then I'm out of your hair. Unless you want to sign my timesheet saying I've completed my time, and we can be done now."

She moved out of the lobby door.

He searched for her Jeep but didn't see it in the parking lot. "Where's your SUV?"

"Oh, you mean my daddy's car." Her voice pitched, and a smug smile crossed her lips. "I was borrowing it." She pointed to the Porsche Cayenne sitting next to his Jeep. "This is my ride."

"Figures."

She pulled on the handle, but it didn't open.

"Dammit." She rummaged through her purse. "Where's the key fob?"

He moved to the passenger side of his Jeep and yanked the door open. "Get in."

"Not on your life." She walked to the hood of her SUV and dumped the contents of her purse. After a thorough search, she growled. "My key is gone."

He pointed to the door. "Just get in. We're heading in the same direction, right?"

"I can drive myself."

He laughed. "You really want to park that Porsche in front of the Soup Kitchen?"

"I've heard that crime has no address." She shoved her stuff back into her purse.

"No, but it's got a zip code. Come on; I'll drive. We're going and returning to the same places."

She huffed but climbed into his Jeep. When he took his place in the driver's seat, she turned to face him.

"Tell me, Officer Rossi, why is it you have so much disdain for the wealthy, and yet, you live in a million-dollar penthouse? I'd say you're a hypocrite. I'd also say Aspen has a very generous compensation package for their police officers."

He pushed the start button and pulled out of the parking lot.

"It's a long story, and the salary isn't all that great."

She tapped her finger on her chin. "Hmm, you drive a Jeep just like my father's, and you live here. I'd say you're doing all right."

He let out a throaty growl. "I live here because Mrs. Mason asked me to move into her rental flat. Having me around made her feel safer after her husband was murdered."

Her breath hitched. "Oh, that's awful."

"Yep, it was awful. A guy knocked Fortney to the pavement and stole the five dollars he had in his pocket. He suffered a brain injury and never recovered. I'm the arresting officer. It took her months to talk me into living there, but she was a kind old lady, and I felt bad for her."

"You felt bad for a billionaire? Seems unlikely to me. Not a bad payoff for you. Do you live there for free?"

"Are you always so judgmental?" He made a right turn and drove the straightaway to the Soup Kitchen.

"Are you? Why is it some rich people are okay, and others are not?"

"Mrs. Mason never used her money to control people."

He glanced over long enough to see her roll her eyes.

"She used it to manipulate you. You sure didn't mind her influence as long as she was paying the bills. Typical."

He pulled behind the building and shoved the gearshift into park. "Geez, whoever he was, he did a number on you. Do you hate all men or just me?"

She shrugged. "I like my brother."

"Lucky him."

She climbed out of the SUV and walked to the door, where she waited for him to unlock it.

"He is lucky. We both are. All we had was each other. Our father was there, but he was simply a visitor who paid the bills and signed our report cards. James and I raised ourselves."

"Well, that explains a lot."

"You're not nice."

"I have a nice side."

"Let me know when it comes out of hiding."

She marched inside the building and hung her purse behind the door. She'd only been here a few days, but she moved around the kitchen like she'd worked there for a lifetime. That was one thing he liked about her. She seemed to adapt easily. Maybe that was because she had to be resilient.

"I think we have ground beef and broccoli. How about meatloaf, mashed potatoes, and steamed veggies?"

She moved to the prep table and leaned on it. "What do you want me to do?"

He quirked a brow. "Can you cook?"

"I'm about as skilled in the culinary arts as you are in kindness."

"Perfect, the hamburger is in the refrigerator. We call it mystery loaf here because it's always different depending on what we have on hand. Have at it."

She pulled a large mixing bowl from under the table and set it on top. She opened the refrigerator only to have the handle come off in her hand again.

"The place is falling apart."

"I do what I can with duct tape and glue."

"How is it funded?"

"We run on a shoestring budget and donations."

"You're lacking in everything." She pointed to the sink where the handle was held together by tape. "Is that up to code?"

He shrugged. "Not sure, the last time they inspected us, the guy walked out to find his tires missing. He hasn't been back."

"Oh my God, I'm so glad I didn't bring my SUV."

"You're welcome."

"For what?" She pulled out several pounds of ground beef and an onion from the cooler.

"For being nice. Saving your car was me being nice."

She walked to the sink and washed her hands. "No, that was you being pushy. Saving my car was a byproduct of your attitude."

"My attitude is a mirror of yours." He grabbed the industrial-sized pan from the shelf overhead and placed it on the stove. They had two jumbo boxes of instant mashed potatoes left. On the shelf, there was a bag of rice, a bag of beans, and enough stuff to make his weekly spaghetti. Because they were using the ground beef tonight, there wouldn't be meatballs tomorrow. It would disappoint Timmy.

"You really don't have a lot here, do you?" She tossed the beef into the bowl and diced the onion.

"If you don't like what you see, do something about it."

"Oh, I get it. You look at me and see a blank check. Typical male."

He stalked toward her. "No, I look at you and see a privileged, spoiled woman with an Ivy League caliber education, but when it comes to people ... you're not all that smart."

Her body shook. "Oh. My. God. I run a multi-billion-dollar resort chain with thousands of employees."

"I'll be impressed when you could run it on donations and volunteers."

She pursed her lips and began dicing. A moment later, tears ran down her cheeks, but he wasn't sure if it was from emotion or the onion.

"Look, Allie, I'm sorry."

She pointed the knife in his direction. "Don't talk to me, or I'm liable to stab you, and then you'll have a great reason to arrest me."

The next two hours passed in silence. Well, ... she was silent to him and jovial to everyone else. She even sat down with Dean and Stu and played a game of rummy. By the looks in their eyes, they were smitten. He got it. She was a pretty attractive woman with a smile that could warm him like the sun on a summer day. Too bad he got the cold shoulder.

After the last person trickled out, and he was starting the dishes, his phone rang.

"Rossi," he answered. "Got it. I'm on my way."

He found her wiping down the tables. "There's a hostage situation, and I need to go." He tossed her the keys and said, "Lock up. I'll see you tomorrow."

She shouted after him, but he was already halfway inside the SUV. He started the engine and took off toward the bank.

It wasn't until an hour later when the crisis was over that he realized he'd driven her to the Soup Kitchen and left her there alone without a way to get home. He raced back but found the place locked up and Allie nowhere in sight. If he thought she was hostile before, he couldn't wait to see what she was like the next time he saw her.

He drove home with every intention of knocking on her door to make sure she was okay, but when he got off the elevator, there was an envelope stuck to the hallway wall labeled "asshole," and inside were the soup kitchen keys.

Chapter 13

How long would she make him suffer? Each time he knocked on her door, she ignored him. Last night, he had left her stranded in hell without a second thought. Not even the cookies and the full-fat, caffeinated latte he left this morning would take the sting away.

Thankfully, she'd gotten to know a few of the locals that hung around the Soup Kitchen. A man they called Slick walked her to the bus station and showed her the route to get to her side of town. She'd never ridden public transportation, but it was appalling and smelled like dog pee and cigarettes. The bus drivers deserved medals for what they put up with.

She sat behind Scott the driver the whole way and listened as he argued with patrons about rate hikes and route stops removed five years ago.

She wanted to scream, "It's been five years, lady. Sit down so it doesn't take another five for me to get home," but she kept her mouth shut. This wasn't her world.

Maybe Marco was right. She had lived a privileged

life and didn't fully understand the plight of the average man. Although she had earned every dollar in her account, she grew up with advantages that some did not, like hot meals, clean clothes, and good medical and dental coverage. She didn't have to worry about where she would sleep or if she'd eat that day.

Yes, she attended the Wharton School of Business, but not because her father paid for it. She paid for it with student loans. One thing that bothered her the most about Marco Rossi was he didn't know her, and he didn't take the time to change that. The minute she showed up in her Jimmy Choos, he thought he had her number. Wasn't she more than the zeros in her bank account?

She flopped onto the end stool by the island and opened the cookbook to the pillow pocket recipe. She pulled together the ingredients to give it another try.

8 oz cream cheese

5 cups all-purpose flour

1 cup granulated sugar

1 1/2 cups filling of your choice. Let your imagination run wild.

1 cup powdered sugar

1 pound real butter

This time she didn't skip the intro to the recipe and began at the top because she obviously missed something. How could a cookie with limited ingredients come out so bad?

Dear Baker,

The first time I came across this recipe, it was in my Aunt Claudia's kitchen. Sam and I had driven to Oklahoma to visit my kin. Mama had passed that year in

March from a bout of flu, and Daddy followed in April. I'm sure he died of a broken heart.

My life had become smaller in so many ways. My parents were gone, and although we had been married for over a year, we didn't have any children. Each time I saw a mother cuddling her child, I wanted to weep. My heart was full, but my arms were empty.

Sam brought me to Aunt Claudia's for a change of scenery. He hoped leaving home for a bit would give me time to rest and relax. Lord bless that man. Mind you, there was no rest or relaxation at Aunt Claudia's farmhouse.

They were up long before the rooster crowed, cleaning stalls, butchering pigs, and collecting eggs. There wasn't time to wallow in self-pity. Aunt Claudia had a brood of children who had children. They were what mama would have called breeders because someone was pregnant all the time, whether it was cousin Delia, cousin Abby or Aunt Claudia herself, who had a baby boy at fifty-five. Even their prize sow was on her fifth litter in three years. This was a passionate house.

"Holy hell," Allie calculated in her head. "That woman was seventy-three when her son turned eighteen. No, thank you." She had dreams of being a mother but didn't want her kids spoon-feeding her and wiping the drool from her chin along with their own children. She continued to read.

While the men worked the farm, Aunt Claudia fed them. With little Claud, named after her, pulling on her apron strings and begging for the teat all day, she was plum tuckered out, so dessert making went to me.

With thoughts of Aunt Claudia's exhaustion, I chose pillow cookies, thinking she could rest her head while I whipped up a batch. How did that turn to passion, you might ask? Well, the first three days I cooked them, they were gone in a lick, and my Sam was too kind and polite to reach into that cookie jar in front of the others, so I hoarded a few just for him.

Now I know, I said that the recipes weren't supposed to be hoarded, but shared. That only goes for the recipes. It's okay to hold back a few cookies for the ones you love.

Funny thing happened that summer. Sam and I would lay in bed eating cookies and making love, and by July I was as pregnant as Mabel the sow, only she gave birth to twelve piglets, and I gave birth to Samuel Matthew Phelps.

I renamed those cookies Passion Pillow Cookies because if everyone wasn't so passionate about gobbling them up, I might not have had to sneak a few into our room, and little Sam Jr. might still be a dream instead of a reality.

So, fill your life up with passion and fill the cookies with something good, too.

Adelaide Phelps

Allie sighed with happiness. Why she hadn't read that before, she couldn't say. Maybe it was because the note was too long, and she didn't want to take the time, but she was glad she'd done so today. There was a lesson here. She wasn't sure what it was, but she'd figure it out.

Until then, she'd make another batch of cookies and hope for better results.

She mixed the dough, and while it cooled in the new

refrigerator, she scrounged through the cupboards to find something to fill them with. Since unsalted, sugar-free peanut butter was out, and she had little in the way of sweets, she pulled out the jar of jelly. When it came to prep time, she put dollops in the center of the pancake-shaped circles of dough, then covered the bottoms with a top and pinched the edges together. After preheating the oven, she tossed them inside.

The windows were open, and she heard the guys next door yelling at the television. Since Marco would be her neighbor and her taskmaster, maybe it was time to offer him an olive branch. She wanted to dislike the man but found it hard to hate someone who made sure they fed kids like Timmy and Holly.

When the cookies finished baking, she pulled them out of the oven. Jelly oozed from between the layers making the pan look like a bubbling, purple murder scene. They weren't pretty, but they smelled good. She plated half of them up and sprinkled them with enough powdered sugar to cover the mess.

After a deep breath for courage and two more for patience, she walked down the hallway and knocked on the door.

Officer Shrek answered. He looked over his shoulder at his balding roommate. "Hey Terry, look who's here, and she's got cookies." He stepped aside. "Come on in, Allie."

She eyed him with suspicion. "You know my name?"

He laughed. "Darlin, you're all we've heard about for a week. That says something because Marco isn't much of a talker."

"He never seems to shut up when he's around me."

"Come on in. I'm Cameron, the good-looking one, and that guy,"—he pointed to the balding man—"is Terry."

She stepped inside the hallway and followed the man to the living room. Glancing around the place, she marveled at how two homes could be so different. Their kitchens shared the same wall, but other than that, there was nothing they had in common. Hers was magazine chic while theirs was man-cave madness.

"Is Marco home?"

"He's at the Soup Kitchen fixing something."

"I thought he only went in on Sundays in the morning to make sauce. Doesn't Lisa take care of serving the meal?"

"That was the plan." He stared at the ball game on the enormous screen. "Things changed."

She glanced at the cookies and sighed. "I brought these over to share." She offered the plate to Cameron. "They aren't pretty to look at, but I'm reasonably sure they're edible."

"I hear cookies aren't your superpower."

Her jaw dropped. "He told you that too?"

"A regular chatterbox lately. Anyway, he said something about a plumbing leak."

"Maybe he should hire skilled labor. The whole place is falling apart around him. You figure if he could live here, he should be able to afford to hire out."

Cameron plucked a cookie from the tray and popped it into his mouth.

She watched his face turn from cautionary to bliss as his powdered sugar smile grew wide.

"Things aren't always what they appear to be. Take these cookies, for instance. They look like hell, but they're good. If I had judged them by how they appeared, they would have ended up in the trash can as soon as you left."

Terry rushed over to grab one. He ate the first in a hurry, and when he deemed them edible, he took three more and went back to watch the game.

She handed over the plate and smiled. "I want that plate back."

Cameron set it down on the table and walked her to the door. "I'll trade it for another plate of treats."

"Not likely. They weren't for you, anyway."

"Are you turning sweet on Marco?"

She shrugged. "No, just trying to sweeten him up, so he's not as sour to me." She turned and walked out the door.

SHE DIDN'T HAVE a shift at the Soup Kitchen today but stopped by, anyway. She found the door unlocked and tugged it open. "Hey," she said, walking inside.

"Holy hell!" Having startled him, Marco jolted up, hitting his head on the underside of the sink. "Make some noise when you come in. You almost gave me a coronary." He grabbed his head and looked at the blood on his fingertips. "Dammit."

"You're bleeding?"

"You think?" He crawled out from under the sink and grabbed a wad of paper towels to press to the injury. "Did they teach you the process of deduction at that fancy college of yours?"

"Did they teach asshattery at the police academy?" She took his elbow and pulled him into the office. "Let me look at you."

He shrugged her off and walked ahead. "I'm fine. It's just a cut."

"I feel responsible, so let me take care of it." She pulled the first-aid kit from the wall and cleaned the wound with an antiseptic wipe.

"That hurts."

"Stop being a baby." She found the silliest Band-Aid in the box. It was pink with yellow daisies. She plastered it over his wound and pressed her lips to it as if he were a child. He was acting like one.

"Why are you here today?" He sat back in the chair, watching her put the kit away.

"Why are you so grumpy?"

"Because I cut my head, and I'm tired, and I'm hungry. Do you need more excuses?"

"You need a break. You do too much, and it's showing in your unpleasant disposition."

"What do you suggest?"

"Is Lisa coming in soon?"

"She'll be here within the hour."

She peeked outside the door into the kitchen. "Will the plumbing hold out for another day?"

"I fixed it. What are you getting at?"

She pulled on his arm. "Let's go." She yanked at him

until he stood and followed her to the sink. She picked up his tools and threw them in the box. "I'm taking you to dinner."

His head snapped back, and he gawked at her. "Are you asking me on a date, Ms. Parks?"

She let out a gut-busting, doubled-over laugh. "In your dreams. I feel bad for causing you injury."

He followed her out the door and locked it behind them.

"Is that why you showed up here on a non-scheduled day? Did you plan to take me to dinner on the off chance that you'd walk in and make me crack my melon open?"

She pointed to the Porsche. "Get in."

He shook his head and winced. "Not on your life." His hand raised to touch the bandage.

"Not my life, but your life, which I'll make more miserable if you don't get in the car." She walked over and opened the passenger door. "Now."

He moved as if he would follow directions but turned around quickly, gripped her shoulders, and pulled her to him. "I'm not dying before I get to kiss you." His hand threaded into the back of her hair while his lips crushed against hers. When she opened her mouth, he dove right in. Even his kisses were combative; their tongues dueled as if fighting for dominance. There was no give and take. They were both taking as much as the kiss would allow.

Hot velvet strokes of his tongue weakened her knees. She reached up and tugged at his hair, holding onto handfuls of it to steady her stance. There was nothing sweet about the kiss. It was angry and lustful and needy and perfect. Every cell in her body came alive.

When he pulled back, she whimpered. They stood there, staring at one another, licking their lips. That kiss was pure unadulterated passion. It stirred a hunger in her that she feared might never be sated.

"Why did you want to kiss me?"

He shrugged. "I needed to know if your kisses were as hot as your temper."

"And?"

"Chernobyl." He bit his lip and shook his head. "Did you say you were taking me to dinner?"

She couldn't take her eyes off his lips. Lips that ignited some dormant need inside her, and it wasn't for food.

"Allie?" He tipped her chin up and forced her to look into his eyes. "You okay?"

"Umm, yes." She cocked her head. "What just happened?"

He chuckled. "We lit the world on fire."

Chapter 14

The quick beat of his heart pulsed through his veins. The force of the pressure throbbed in the cut to his forehead. He pulled the visor down and looked at the ridiculous flowered Band-Aid she'd patched him up with. She could have used the plain one, but everything with Allie was a challenge, and it appeared he liked defiance.

"Really? Flowers."

She pulled out of the parking lot and onto the street.

"It's a good look on you. I'd say it softens your hardness."

He thought of a few comebacks referring to hardness. After that kiss, his mind was muddled, and his body primed for passion, but he bit his tongue. One thing he'd learned from his mom was thoughts should be filtered before they became words.

"I'm not wearing this to dinner with you."

She glanced over and scowled. "You're not taking it off in my car. You'll make it bleed, and it will get everywhere."

He flipped the visor closed. "Watch the road."

"Stop bossing me around. I'm a good driver."

"I'm surprised you have a license from what I've seen."

"Is this verbal sparring between us your version of foreplay?"

When he thought of foreplay, it started with flowers and included tactile exploration. "Do you think your sassy mouth is sexy?"

"You didn't seem to mind my mouth a few minutes ago."

She was right. He rather enjoyed the kiss. His brain and body were still reeling from the experience. He wasn't usually so impulsive. In his job, he had to think on his feet, but there was no thinking when he pulled her to him for that kiss. Logically, he could tell himself that he kissed her to shut her up, but truthfully, he'd been thinking about those lips since that first day she showed at the Soup Kitchen in a snug skirt and heels.

"Where are we going?"

A sly smile lifted the corners of her lips. "I've had to endure your world. Don't you think it's time you see mine?"

"Can't wait."

"You're such a grump."

She whipped the Porsche around the corner and drove down the block to Luxe. He would have liked to give her a hard time for her driving skills, but she was a good driver. While historically she drove with a lead foot; she didn't push past the speed limit once.

She pulled down the ramp of the underground

garage and slid into a spot reserved for the chief operating officer.

"Reserved parking—fancy."

She killed the engine and reached into the back seat for her purse. "I bet you get premium parking anywhere you go. All you have to do is flash your lights."

He exited and rushed around to open her door. "I never take advantage of my power as a police officer."

"Really? I'd totally turn on my lights if it got me where I wanted to be sooner."

"That's why I wear the badge, and you don't. Besides, while you're rushing to get from point A to point B, you're missing everything in between."

"Says the man who works himself to death between the Soup Kitchen and the police department."

"Today, you're rescuing me."

They walked side by side to the elevator. After she pushed the button, she reached up and tore the Band-Aid off in one quick tug.

"Ouch!"

"You're such a baby." She grabbed the collar of his shirt and tugged him down, so she was eye-to-eye with the wound. "You'll live." She pressed her lips to the cut for a gentle kiss.

"That definitely makes it feel better."

"Glad I could help." The elevator door opened, and they stepped inside.

"Allie, I'm kissing you again." He moved closer until his chest grazed hers. The current passing between them grew. "It's probably not wise, but I can't help myself."

She lifted on her tiptoes and pressed her lips to his.

"It's probably the head injury. Kiss me now because I'm sure tomorrow you'll come to your senses and return to your usual surly self."

It was a quick kiss that only lasted the time it took the elevator to rise one floor. When the doors opened, she walked off as if nothing had happened, but something had. She had gotten to him. He couldn't explain it, but he wanted it to happen again.

They moved past the front desk.

"Good evening Allie," said the male behind the counter. The young man beamed at her like he was in love. "Do you need anything?"

"No thanks, I'm taking a friend to dinner."

He rushed around the counter and followed them. "Oh, should I call Flynn and let him know you're on your way?"

"I'll get there before you would reach him. Have a good night, Scott."

Allie giggled. It was a sweet, bubbly sound that warmed his heart. Had he been the reason for her upswing in mood, or was it the young man following them? He'd never been the jealous type, but he'd just gotten a taste of the passionate side of Allie, and he wasn't ready to let her go. Scott better be careful because he wasn't willing to share his new bone.

He felt bad thinking about Allie as a possession, comparing her to a bone, but he felt as protective of her as a pit bull would his master. That meant he was the dog, and Allie, the master, and he wasn't sure he liked that.

He'd fallen behind, so he rushed to her side. As they walked through the lobby to a restaurant called The

Lodge, several other people greeted her like she was royalty. He imagined they treated her like that because she was part owner.

After they'd had their blowout, and she'd told him she ran ten resorts, he put his investigative skills to work and googled her. There were three owners: Allie, James, and someone named Julian. Her net worth was astronomical, but he imagined her money was tied up in investments. Even though that might be true, she was wealthy by most standards.

"This is The Lodge. We're working on the menu, but it will be the gold nugget to our success. People can forgive a lumpy pillow but never a bad meal."

They walked inside and passed the host who scurried behind them with menus.

The restaurant was lodge chic. Huge antler chandeliers hung from open beamed ceilings while the walls had inlaid wood depicting mountains.

He breathed deeply and took in the smells of smoked meat and something sweet.

Allie walked through the doors of a private dining area and headed for a small table for two.

"Can you tell Flynn or Molly that we're here?"

"Yes, ma'am." The host whose name tag read Blaine, rushed out, leaving them alone.

"You're like royalty here." He pulled out her chair and took the one across from her.

"It's not about me at all, but about the fact that my name is one of three that signs their checks. People aren't all that genuine when there's money or power in a relationship."

"Isn't money power on its own?"

She opened the menu and looked at the offerings. "I suppose it's how you use it."

"Tell me how you got started in the business."

She had just opened her mouth when a man dressed in a chef's jacket arrived.

"Allie, you should have told me you were coming. I could have prepared something special."

She smiled, but he could see it wasn't genuine. There was no shine in her eyes or a blush to her cheeks.

"I want to see what our guests see and eat what they eat. I can't get a good feel for what's real if I'm dining from a special menu."

She looked down at the offerings and then at Marco. "Would you like to sample a bunch of things? We can get the tasting menu?"

"It's your call, sweetheart."

Flynn's brow hiked high on his forehead. "Sweetheart?"

Heat rose to pink Allie's cheeks. "Sorry, that was rude of me not to introduce my friend, Marco Rossi."

"Nice to meet you." Flynn shook his hand firmly and gave him a once over as if he were vetting his suitability. "Tasting menu, then?"

"Sounds fabulous."

"Wine too?"

She shook her head. "Not for me. I'm driving." She nodded toward Marco. "This one would have me in cuffs if I acted recklessly."

"Kinky."

Marco smiled. That wasn't a vision he would have

plucked from the air, but now he wouldn't be able to get it out of his head.

"None for me either. How about an iced tea?"

Flynn picked up the menus. "Doesn't pair as well as the Duckhorn I would have suggested, but it will do." He disappeared, leaving them alone once again.

"Are we?" he asked Allie.

She unrolled her silverware and placed the napkin on her lap. "Are we what?"

He reached across the table to take her hand. "Are we friends?"

She seemed to ponder that for a moment. "I'm not sure what we are, but if being friends gets me more of those kisses." She lifted her shoulders. "I'm game to try friendship."

"That sounds like an excellent idea. More kisses that is. Now that we're friends, tell me how you got started."

She told him about their posh vacations, prior to her parents' divorce, and how she and James would make lists of improvements they would do if they were in charge. She talked about college and moving from location to location.

"You were a nomad, but now you're settling down?"

"It's important to realize when you have enough."

He smiled. "My mom used to tell me that you never needed more than enough, but I haven't reached that metric yet."

"Tell me about the Soup Kitchen and how it became your responsibility."

The tea came with their first course, which was a

pear and goat cheese salad. He took a bite and thought about where to begin.

"Remember when I told you that Judge Matthews lost his best friend because of a reckless driver?"

She swallowed and stared at him. It was as if she knew what he would say before the words spilled out. A tear ran down her cheek.

He nodded. "That was my father, and he died along with my mother."

She dropped her fork. "I'm so sorry. Did the guy go to jail?"

"He did, but he tried to buy his way out of the sentence. He thought his money could solve the problems. It turned out the only one who benefited from his wealth was his legal team. I tried to sue him after the fact hoping to keep the Soup Kitchen open, but there was nothing left."

"You keep it open for your mom?"

He leaned back and closed his eyes. Each time he tried to picture his mom in his mind, her image became fuzzier.

"It's her legacy. I spent a lot of time there when I was a kid. Before my father joined the police force, he was a plumber." He touched his head. "Before you say it, I know it's not my superpower. Anyway, he had a hard time finding work, and when things were tight, we ate there. Only then, someone else ran it. They ran out of funds and were going to close the place, but my mom took over, and the rest is history. No matter how bad things were or how bad things got, she always put a meal on the table."

She sat for a minute before she swiped the tear from her cheek. "That's why you have such disdain for the wealthy."

"I just hate that people are treated differently because they have money."

"I didn't expect different treatment."

"Might I remind you that you tried to manipulate me out of a ticket?"

She tapped the table with her index finger. "That had nothing to do with money; I just didn't want a ticket. I couldn't afford one. I didn't ask for special treatment because of my wealth."

He set his fork on his plate and pushed it away. "If I had said I'd walk away for a hundred bucks, would you have given it to me?"

"Yes."

At least she was honest.

"I would have given you a thousand, but I didn't bribe you."

"Did you consider it?"

Her head fell, and he knew she had.

"I did, but it was because there was the real possibility that I'd lose my license."

"Yeah, well, the guy who killed my parents was heading to a fundraiser, and my parents' lost their lives."

She reached across the table to hold his hand. Her thumb brushed over his knuckles. "I'm so sorry. I really am. I understand why you're angry. After hearing your story, I'm mad at myself for being reckless. You're right. I could have hurt someone. When you're in the moment, you don't think about the consequences, and that makes me a selfish person."

"I have a feeling you're used to getting what you want." He looked toward the door where Flynn arrived with another course. This one was a kind of soup. He mentioned something about carrots and turmeric and left. "Do you think people would worship you if you were broke?"

Her nose wrinkled when she frowned. "No one worships me."

"That's the problem with your wealth, Allie. You're used to it and don't see the special treatment you get. If you didn't have the wealth you do, no one would greet you like they did when you entered the resort. The Gucci and Prada you wear make the saleswomen downtown rush to you for a commission, but put someone in a pair of Walmart jeans and it would be a different story. Your wealth is your power."

"What about your wealth? You drive a nice car and live in a penthouse in the same building as me."

"Things aren't always what they seem."

"Then explain to me how things are."

"Mrs. Mason's will gave me a year to find another place. Her son can sell anytime, but the new owner would have to let me live there for next to nothing until the agreement is up. I don't own the place. I have room-mates, so I can afford to keep the Soup Kitchen open." He sipped his tea and let the cool liquid wash down the bitter truth. "You and I are not the same. You could write a check and make everything all right. Me? I get room-mates, beg and borrow, and do my own plumbing."

"No, you're right. We're not alike. When I look at you, I see a capable, but cantankerous man. When you look at me, you see dollar signs like every other asshole I've dated."

"You're wrong."

"No, I'm not. Don't punish me for being rich."

He picked up his napkin and laid it on the table. "Don't punish me because of how others see you. Your money is the least attractive thing about you." He pulled out several twenties from his pocket and tossed it next to his plate before he stood and walked out of the room.

Chapter 15

"He got up and left," Allie said. "He took his napkin from his lap, tossed it on the table, and left."

Dani rolled her chair forward.

They were sitting in the conference room Monday morning, going over the latest profit-and-loss numbers. At this point, the resort was at a loss and would be for years to come, but things appeared to be on track. At least with the suites renovated and several upper floors complete, they could open rooms for reservations.

"I'm still at the part where he kissed you. Let's go back to that."

"What's there to go back to? He kissed me. Three times or maybe it was two. Hell, he made my head so foggy it could have been four. I'm not sure."

Dani, with her mouth slightly open, and her eyes narrowed, cocked her head to the side. "Was it a good kiss?"

Allie growled in frustration. "It doesn't matter. He and I are oil and water."

Dani leaned back in her chair, kicked out her feet, and crossed them at her ankles. She was getting comfortable, which meant the talk about Marco wouldn't end anytime soon.

"Last time you said you were gunpowder, and he was the spark. I told you there was chemistry there. I haven't seen you this riled in a while." She pointed to the double shot mocha on the table. "He's got you drinking caffeine and sugar. That means something."

She shook her head. "You're too much of a romantic. All it means is I'm tired of his bullshit, hence the caffeine to wake me up, and I needed sugar to erase the bitterness of his kisses from my tongue."

"Just a minute ago, you said his kisses made you feel woozy."

"No, I said foggy, and I hate the fog." Who was she kidding? She liked his kisses. If that's all they did together, she was game, but he was the most frustrating man she'd ever met. When she didn't want to kiss him, she wanted to clobber him over the head with a wrench from his toolbox.

"You like him, and that's why you're so upset." Dani pulled in her legs and rolled her chair closer to Allie. "Tell me the truth. You're hurt because he walked out on you. What happened that made him feel like that was his only recourse?"

She closed her eyes and replayed the minutes in her mind. "I accused him of seeing me as a dollar sign."

Dani jumped up and walked to the window. "Geez, I get that money is an issue with you guys, but some people don't really give a damn about it. I wouldn't care if your brother was a pauper or a prince. I love him. Frankly, I think you're more hung up about the money than Marco is. Maybe you inherited that from your mother."

That thought made bile rise into Allie's throat. She swallowed the burn of Dani's statement. "I'm not anything like my mother. I've got money, but it's not the focus of my life. If it were gone tomorrow, I'd figure out a way to survive."

"Has he asked you for anything?"

"It's not that. He just doesn't like wealthy people. He's had some run-ins with some unsavory ones, and it's made him jaded."

"We're all jaded about something. I don't like slimy exes who take me to the cleaners. Chris was the worst. He was dishonest, manipulative, a cheater, and a dirty scoundrel in every sense of the word. I was distrustful of all men for a time, and then your brother came along, and guess what? He wasn't honest. Most people would have kicked him to the curb, but you told me to give him another chance. I did because you convinced me that not all men are shits."

"My brother is an amazing man."

"I agree, but do you know why Marco has a dislike for the ultra-wealthy? Seems to me there is something deep-seated in his resentment."

She told Dani the tragedy that surrounded Marco. "I get it, but I'm not like the guy who killed his parents."

"Are you sure? He clocked you going twenty miles over the speed limit. Even you told me you swerved into the oncoming lane because something distracted you. You could have easily been that guy. Since you're convinced that you're not that person, maybe you need to cut him some slack and consider that he might not be who you think either. He hasn't asked you for anything."

"But he needs so much. That Soup Kitchen is falling apart at the seams. The shelves are empty. To say he runs it on a skimpy budget is generous."

"That doesn't mean he expects you to save him. Take me, for instance. I'm buried in debt. Even if your brother wanted to write a check to bail me out, I've got way too much pride to let him. I'm in this mess because of my decisions, and I'll get myself out."

"Why hasn't he asked me for help?"

Dani laughed. "You can't have it both ways. You can't be upset that he didn't ask and then hate him if he did. Choose your side. I imagine he's a prideful man, and keeping the Soup Kitchen open is a way to keep the memory of his parents alive."

"You're right. I just need to relax and let it go."

Dani walked back and leaned over to hug her. "Everything you're going through is so tied up in your childhood and past relationships. Your mother didn't do you any favors by leaving and taking everything. It showed you and your brother that she didn't value either of you, just money. The same goes for the asshole who hurt you." She took her seat again and touched her chin. "Funny how you both amassed so much of what they valued. Do you think there's some Freudian reason for that? As for your mother, are you hoping she'll come back —that somehow what you've saved will bring her back to you?"

Allie's heart felt hollow. She'd never considered why

it was so important for them to succeed. Was it truly to prove that she was worthy of her mother's love?

"I don't know what to say."

"Well, consider this. Maybe it's not that you're unworthy of her, but that she's not worthy of you. As for Marco, he's not your mom; he's not your ex. He hasn't taken anything from you."

"Not true. He stole my kisses."

"I'm going to call bullshit. I bet you gave them freely."

"You're right. I was shocked at first, but I didn't push him away. In fact, I'm sure I tugged him forward, but now what? I'm everything he likes and despises. He told me my money was the least attractive thing about me."

"Sounds to me like he's perfect for you."

"No, I'll never not be wealthy. I'm too good at what I do to fail."

"Even the playing field."

"Are you asking me to give it all up?"

"Not at all. Obviously, you like him. I'd even say you care about him. You guys have a spark. Sure, you may be gunpowder, and he's the flame, but when there's that kind of explosive passion, I'd say it's worth investigating. He never asked for your help, but what if you gave it to him before he asked?"

"He would never take anything from me now."

Dani gathered the reports and put them in a folder. "You have more resources than money. Use them."

"I've got a lot to think about."

Dani reached out and covered her hand. "I think best when I'm baking. There's so much time in between the mixing and the finished product that it gives me a chance to consider the ingredients in my life."

"Are we back to that cookbook you know nothing about?"

Dani beamed. "Let's pretend that I know a bit about it. Did you read the entire recipe? I hadn't initially, and that was my first mistake. The second was when I decided I knew better than the woman who wrote it. I substituted ingredients. I didn't respect the process. Nothing truly came together until I sat down and really looked at it. The same was true with my life, and my love for James."

Allie rubbed at her temples, trying to massage her headache away. "There's a lesson there that I'm missing."

"Go home and start from the beginning. Sometimes, when I'm lost, I go back to the start to figure out where I got off track."

Allie stood and pressed out the wrinkles in her skirt. "Do you even know who Adelaide Phelps was?"

Dani walked with her to the door. "Who?"

"You know ... Adelaide, the woman who wrote the cookbook."

"What cookbook?" Dani winked and walked down the hall toward her office.

Allie gathered her things and headed home. When she got there, Marco's Jeep wasn't anywhere in sight.

She changed her clothes and headed to the Soup Kitchen. Dani was right about many things. There was a spark, but there was also a lot of underlying wounds that needed healing. They could never move past a kiss if they constantly wanted to kill each other. She was also right about resources. Money wasn't all that she had in her toolbox. She had connections.

She made a few calls, called in a few favors, and walked into the Soup Kitchen.

She stood in the doorway and watched Marco work under the sink. Not wanting to startle him, she cleared her throat.

He twisted his body to look her way, and he smiled. The man smiled, and any uneasiness she felt walking into the kitchen disappeared.

"I wasn't sure you'd come in after last night."

She shrugged. "It would seem I'm a glutton for punishment."

He shimmied out from under the sink and moved toward her. "I'm glad you came because I wanted to tell you that I'm sorry. I wasn't at my best." He shoved his hands into his pockets and rocked back and forth. The image of big, bad Marco Rossi feeling intimidated by her presence was satisfying. His shy and uncertain demeanor made her feel ten feet tall.

"Me too." She reached up and gently touched the cut on his forehead. "How's it feeling?"

He hung his head. "It would feel so much better if you kissed me."

Chapter 16

"Don't push your luck, buddy. I don't kiss people who don't like me."

He gripped her shoulders and held her there so she couldn't escape. "Seems to me like you already kissed me, and you didn't have exacting standards then."

She squirmed, but only stepped closer. Her behavior might resemble disinterest, but her actions were exactly the opposite.

"If my memory serves me correctly, I believe *you* kissed me." She stood as tall as she could and set her chin higher in defiance. "My standards haven't changed."

"Allie Parks, you drive me batshit crazy."

"And you make me want to commit capital murder."

"That's not a wise thing to tell an officer of the law. How about I forget that I heard your murderous confession and kiss you instead?"

"Officer Rossi, stop talking, and just do it."

He waited for a long second and stared into her eyes. There was a swirling mass of emotions in those green pools; flecks of fiery amber, a sea of calming green, and onyx so black that he wasn't sure if it represented her soul, or her heart, or her emptiness. Allie was a volatile mix of pain-in-the-ass and passion. He liked everything about her and nothing at the same time.

That's not true; I like everything about her, but I know she's all wrong for me in the right way.

He bent his head and nipped at her plump lower lip.

She inched closer until they were chest to chest. Only the cotton of their T-shirts separated them. When he pulled her lip into his mouth and sucked on it, she groaned. Every cell in his body responded to that sound. It was full of need and want and desire.

When he covered her mouth with his, she opened willingly as if she was just as hungry as he was to feel something other than the status quo.

Her kisses tasted of peppermint and passion. They promised everything and nothing at the same time.

Their tongues tangled, and his hands skimmed her body from her shoulders to her hips. He walked her back and trapped her between the wall and him. Her body vibrated against his, reaching and pressing into him until he was on fire. The hard length of him pressed high on her belly. She didn't seem to mind. It was almost as if she reveled in the feel of him with the way she moved against him.

He reached down and gripped her bottom, lifting her until she wrapped her legs around his waist. That nearly undid him. His heat was at her core, and the only thing stopping them from something they'd regret was a quarter-inch of denim that sat between them.

"You're killing me."

"Shut up and keep kissing me." She wrapped her arms around his neck and pulled him tighter.

"Are you always this bossy?" He whispered against her lips.

"Sometimes, I'm worse."

A bubble of laughter rose from his stomach, to his chest, to his mouth. She'd just thrown his words back at him, and he liked it. He liked her fire and her snarky attitude. He liked that she was a woman who gave as much as she took. With the way her hips ground against his, he knew she'd give a lot in that department.

Behind them, the door opened, and the outside light shined on them like a spotlight. He let her slip from his hands. As soon as her feet hit the floor, he moved back.

He didn't dare face whoever came into the kitchen. There was way too much exposed for him to be comfortable with that. Instead, he painfully moved back to the sink and crawled under it to finish the job he started.

"Can you hand me a wrench?" His hand thrust out, hoping Allie would play along. When she didn't, he took a peek to see who had come in.

Seeing Lisa made all passion he'd felt for Allie leave his body. It wasn't because he didn't like her. He just didn't like her in the same way. She was a good twenty years older than him, and life had not been kind to her. Years of living on the street had taken its toll, and she appeared closer to seventy than she did to her late fifties.

"Hey, Lisa. I'm just finishing up here on the sink. Allie was helping me find the wrench." He shook his hand again while Allie, who stood nearby looking mortified, did nothing.

Lisa reached down to the toolbox and picked up the crescent wrench. "I saw you looking for it. I don't think you'll find it in her mouth." She laughed and walked toward the office.

He gave the pipe fitting another twist and moved out from under the sink.

Allie fisted up and punched him in the arm. She looked toward the office and whispered, "You left me standing here all by myself." The back of her hand came up to wipe her kiss-swollen lips. "She knows what we've been doing."

He released a sigh and leaned forward until his lips grazed her lips. "I was surprised too, but really, what do we have to be embarrassed about?"

"I'm like your employee."

He shook his head. "Not even close. You're more like a parolee." He moved until she was pinned against the wall again. "Hey Lisa, I need to kiss Allie again, okay."

"Just stay off the prep-table. We need to keep things hygienic in here. We've got enough problems that we don't need the health department on our ass too." She kicked the door closed, and he deepened the kiss.

It wasn't until a pounding at the door echoed through the room that he pulled away. "I'd like a repeat of that later."

She opened the refrigerator, and the handle came off in her hand. "If you take care of me like you do this place, I'm in trouble."

He whipped around and stalked toward her. "Honey,

when I take care of you, you'll completely fall to pieces." He chuckled at the look of surprise on her face. When the pounding at the door sounded again, Lisa yelled from the office. "Can't you stop sucking face for a second to answer the door?"

He pressed a quick kiss to her lips and spun around to walk toward the door. When he answered it, there was a man wearing a Luxe Resorts uniform.

"Can I help you?" He glanced over his shoulder to Allie.

She rushed forward. "Todd, thanks for coming over." She put a finger in the belt loop of Marco's pants and pulled him aside so the man she called Todd could enter. "This is Marco. He runs the Soup Kitchen." She pointed to the office. "Lisa is in there."

Marco cocked his head to the side. "Is there a reason *Todd* is here?"

Todd smiled at Allie. "I heard you could use a little help."

He didn't like the way the man looked at Allie; it was like he was half in love with her—in love with his girl. Not that it was a given that Allie was his, but that kiss made it feel like they were together. That kiss was the best thing that happened to him since the last kiss they shared.

How funny was it that a kiss from a woman who barely tolerated him could be the highlight of his day—his week—his month. He didn't understand how, but Allie was like water in the desert, the sun after a blizzard, and rain after a drought.

"I thought it might be good to get a professional here

to give the place a once over." She stared at the scabbed-over cut on his forehead. "It's time for us to use my head and not yours to figure out some repairs."

The word 'us' warmed him, but at the same time, he felt offended that she might consider him inept to do repairs.

"I've been doing okay."

She still held the handle to the refrigerator in her hand. "Yes, I'm sure,—" she set the handle in his palm,— "you're an excellent DIY man, but Todd was free today, and I thought you might like him to look over the place to see what it needs to bring it into the twentieth century."

He scowled, "It's the twenty-first century."

Her eyes brightened, and her lips curled into a smile. "I know, but we can't move you too fast from the iron age to civilization. The shock would kill you."

"Haha." He offered his hand to Todd. "Nice to meet you. Are you here to work or tell me what will fall apart next?"

"Both. I'd like to see the sink first." He stared at the handle in Allie's hand. "Then I'll look at the refrigeration unit. If it's all right with you, I'll give the other equipment a glance too. I oversee Luxe, which wasn't so Luxe before Allie, James, and Julian took over. I'm an expert at making things work. There's a limitless number of things a person can do with duct tape and paperclips."

He looked down at Allie, whose lips were still red and swollen with his kisses. "I can't pay you much, but I can feed you a meal if you're around come dinnertime."

Allie pushed the handle into Todd's hand. "Can you

start with this? I can't get into the cooler to see what we're serving for dinner if I can't open it."

"You got it."

Marco placed his hand at the curve of her back and led her into the dining room where they could be alone.

"I wasn't trying to guilt you into helping. I've been doing okay for the last ten years on my own."

She crossed her arms and made a face that scrunched her nose. "Can you just thank me? It's really easy. You stick your tongue to the top of your front teeth and begin with the th sound, then follow it with ank and you."

"I bet you were a handful when you were a teen."

"Hardly, James and I raised ourselves. Dad was working to pay the rent, keep us in school, and pay alimony. We had a little help around the house, but mostly, I ran it. My brother fixed everything, and Dad paid the bills."

He hadn't considered that she might have had a rough life. He knew better than to judge people, but somehow, he'd failed with Allie and let his observations about superficial stuff sour his opinion. He needed to stick with the innocent until proven guilty philosophy.

"Thank you for your help, Allie. You didn't need to send someone here to fix stuff, but you did, and I'm grateful." He hated to admit that he was in over his head. It hurt his pride to know he was barely treading water when it came to the Soup Kitchen. "I can't afford to pay him, but I will feed him."

"Not everyone is interested in money."

"You're right. It's rare that I see someone who wants to help because she can. You're a surprise, Ms. Parks."

"A good surprise or a bad one?"

"That jury is still out." He wrapped his arm around her shoulder and walked her to the door leading to the kitchen. "Shall we make something delicious for the masses?"

"What's on the menu?"

They worked side by side, preparing chicken parmesan over leftover pasta. Lisa stayed in the office, no doubt trying to turn red ink to black.

Todd was a miracle worker. He fixed the handle with a paperclip and duct tape and ended the dripping pipe with plumber's tape and PVC glue.

When it was time to feed everyone, Marco told Allie to open the doors.

It was a simple act, but she bounced with excitement. "Really?"

"You didn't win the lottery; I'm just asking you to let them in."

"I know, but it seems like you're sharing something real and personal with me."

He was. He was sharing his passion, his life, and his legacy. And for the first time in a long time, his heart felt full.

Todd didn't stay for dinner, but he left a list as long as Marco's forearm of things that needed repair or replacement. It was a brutal reminder of the long and tough road ahead.

He stretched his neck and rocked it from side to side to get the kinks out.

"I feel like it's always one step forward and two back."

She walked over and wrapped her arms around his waist. "Let's go home. I can sweeten up your evening."

He looked down at her and raised a brow. "What did you have in mind?"

She laughed. "Cookies, silly. I thought we could make something sweet together."

Chapter 17

Allie rushed home to get things ready for cookie baking. Once all the ingredients were on the counter minus the filling, she went to her bedroom to change. Cooking didn't require a special outfit, but she wanted to look nice for Marco.

Her closet was filled with professional clothes from suits to skirts and silk blouses. Everything was organized by color. A tiny section in the back of her closet held her casual stuff. How sad was it that a section about two feet wide was all she had?

"I really need to get out more." She rummaged through the offerings to find two sundresses, one of which she'd worn to court. There was another pair of jeans and a couple pairs of yoga pants. She wasn't sure what the evening had in store. Did she want more from Marco?

A shiver rippled through her body. She definitely wanted more, but how much more? If she were honest with herself, they were poorly suited for each other, and the only time they got along was when they were kissing. *I am definitely up for more kissing.*

Not wanting to make it obvious that she dressed up for him by wearing a sundress, she changed into a pair of black yoga pants and an off the shoulder tunic.

A tap at the door set her heart racing. He would be the first man she invited into her home outside of her brother. Even Julian hadn't been over to visit, and he was like family.

Barefoot, she nearly skipped down the hallway to the door. When she swung it open, Marco stood there with flowers and a bottle of wine.

"Come in." She shifted to the side to make room for him.

He stared down at the gifts he brought. "My mother taught me never to go anywhere empty-handed."

He offered her the flowers, which she took and brought them to her nose. It was a mixed bouquet with a bit of everything.

"Thank you. Come in." She led him down the hallway to the kitchen. "Let me put these in water. You can open the wine." She took a vase and two glasses from the cupboard and placed them on the island. "The opener is in the top right-hand drawer."

"Wow, the place looks amazing." He turned in a slow circle, taking it all in. "It's just the kitchen you remodeled, but what a difference."

She trimmed the flowers and put them in the vase. "My brother is a miracle worker, and I get a family discount, which is free."

He poured them each a glass of wine and brought hers to her.

"To family discounts and new neighbors."

She raised her glass and said, "To hot neighbors who kiss the strength out of me."

He chuckled. "To that."

They clicked glasses and took a sip.

"You have excellent taste in wine."

He leaned against the counter and looked at the baking ingredients on display.

"I'm Italian. It's a birth requirement to know wine and pasta sauce."

She rubbed her tummy. "I have to say, the chicken parmesan was amazing. If word gets out about how good it is, the Soup Kitchen will be overrun by everyone regardless of need."

He moved toward her like a panther slinking toward its prey. "Which was better, the meal or the kisses?"

She liked this side of Marco—the playful side. "I don't know. That meal was fabulous. Since there isn't any left, I can't do a side-by-side analysis."

"I can't offer you more chicken parmesan, but I can offer a second helping of kisses." He set his glass down and moved the items on the counter to the side. Swiftly, he lifted her, sitting her on the stone top.

Moving forward, he pressed himself between her knees and got as close as the counter would allow. "Then again, maybe you've had enough of my kisses."

She tapped her chin. "Maybe."

"What I'm thinking," he said against her lips, "is that you need another taste to be certain." Not giving her time

141

to think or respond, his mouth pressed against her. He tormented her lips for several minutes with perfect kisses.

The connection between them was undeniable. To hell with the cookies and the wine. She could live on his kisses alone.

Her hand moved up his chest to circle his neck and travel down his back. She swore she could feel his muscles move under her fingertips as if they were reaching and rolling for her touch. She moved to his arms and explored the corded muscles that stretched and strained to get closer to her.

He pulled away and sucked in a breath. "That's the best I got." He stepped back and cocked his head. "More chicken parmesan or kisses?"

"Kisses." She reached out to grab him and pull him back into her arms, but he took another step away.

"All things are better when consumed in moderation." He walked forward and lifted her from the counter to the floor and then turned to line the ingredients back up. "Where do we start?"

She took a few cleansing breaths and the deep ache in her core that tingled and tortured her while they kissed subsided.

"You're an awful tease."

"I don't know about that, but my mom used to tell me I was plain awful."

She took out the bowls they would need and set them next to the ingredients. "I would have liked to meet your mom. I mean, who else would have given me the dirty details about you?"

He leaned against the counter while she measured out the cups of flour. "You can ask my sister Roxanne."

"You have a sister?"

"Yep, she lives in DC and runs the World Food Bank."

This whole feeding the masses was a family thing. "Another Rossi do-gooder."

He turned around and looked at the page of the cookbook she was following and helped measure the ingredients.

"I think coming from an Italian family, food is important. More so than with others. Sundays at any old-school Italian family home was about food and family. My grandmother had a table that sat twenty. It wasn't fancy, just wooden planks strapped together. No one cared what it looked like because when it was covered with food, it was beautiful."

"You ate at your grandparents' house every Sunday?"

He nodded. "We gathered as a family. Everyone would bring something. We didn't have enough family to fill that table, but there was always a seat for someone who wanted to join, and they did. Sometimes it was a neighbor, and there were always friends. Occasionally, there was a stranger or two. Food breaks down barriers. Good food is the universal language of love. Especially if it's shared."

"I can see why keeping the soup kitchen is so important to you."

He took the bowl and began stirring the wet and dry ingredients together.

"The kitchen is everything to me. It was part of my

past. It helped get me through the loss of my parents, and it's a big part of my future. I may get frustrated with the process, but just because it's a challenge doesn't mean it's not worth the effort. I'm not a quitter."

She hip-checked him. "Me either. That's why we're here making these damn cookies again. The peanut butter was a fail, but the jelly ones seemed okay. I brought them over to your roommates. Did they say anything about them? Tell the truth."

He turned to look at her. Something danced in his eyes. It was as if the amber specks were laughing and couldn't stay still. "They said the flavor was good, but they were as flat as a board. If you're calling them pillow cookies, there better be something filling them up."

"You have ungrateful roommates."

"You wanted the truth."

"The recipe doesn't say what to put in them. I've been experimenting."

"What about jam? It's thicker and has chunks of fruit. The problem with jelly is that it liquefies once it gets hot."

Under her breath, she said, "Yep, so do I. One kiss, and I'm a hot mess."

"What was that?"

He heard her. The grin on his face told her so.

"Could it be that easy?"

He moved closer and tugged her into his arms. "Not everything has to be hard."

She giggled. "I like hard."

"Now who's being the tease?"

"All is fair in love and war."

He moved his mouth to her ear. "Allie, do you want to make love or war?"

Her entire body shuddered while he nipped at her neck, licked at her earlobes, and nibbled on her collarbone.

"Are you teasing or asking?"

"Does it matter?"

She leaned back to look in his eyes.

"I don't want you to think I'm easy."

His laughter filled the air. "Oh, sweetheart, no one would ever call you easy."

Her hand ran down the front of his jeans. "But I'd say you could be hard."

He leaned down to sweep her legs into his arms. "Let me show you." He moved down the hallway until he reached the master bedroom but stopped before he entered. "Yes or no. Are you in or out?"

"In, totally in."

He moved inside her room until they reached the bed. She half expected him to toss her on the comforter and ravage her like a caveman, but he laid her down gently.

"What about the cookies?"

"What cookies," she asked. They could rot on the counter for all she cared.

"You're beautiful, Allie. I'm sure you hear that a lot, but I want you to hear me say it."

Her heart turned into melted jelly.

"I don't hear it at all. Most men find me intimidating."

He tugged his shirt off, grasping the hem and pulling it over his head.

It was like watching a present unwrap itself.

"You're beautiful." She rose to explore his chest with her hands and her eyes. It was the first time she'd seen him bare-chested. She could watch this clip of her life on repeat forever.

He reached down and pulled her shirt off. She wasn't self-conscious of her small breasts. It did no good to beat yourself up for how nature made you. The only way her boobs would grow was through plastic surgery, and she had more important things to worry about than that.

As his hands explored her body, she relaxed back into the comforter, and everywhere he touched lit her on fire.

As his thumb grazed the pink buds of her breasts, an involuntary moan left her lips. "Geez, I forgot what this was like."

He rolled to his side and looked at her. "Been awhile?"

A blush crept up her chest to her cheeks. "Not that it's any of your business, but yes, it's been a while. What about you?"

He squinted, and she could almost see the cogs turning in his head. "A very long time. I'm selective. There are certain criteria a woman has to meet."

"Breathing and willing?"

"Yes, that too, but there has to be more. I've had my share of frivolous sex, and honestly, it's not all that satisfying. You make me feel something different, and that's why I'm here."

"Rage and irritation turn you on? Noted."

146

He placed his hand on her hip and shifted, so they were touching. "You definitely bring those two attributes to the table, but it's more."

"You like me." She giggled like a kid. "You really like me." She narrowed her eyes in his direction. "Why?"

"Because you're a challenge, and you're a good person. All you needed to do was show up, but you did more than that. You engaged, and you care. We have more in common than you think."

"But you hate my money."

He shook his head. "No, I hate what money does to people. I thought you were like most others, but you're not. You don't use it to manipulate."

She rolled her eyes. "Oh, but I do. I bribed the linen guy with money to provide better quality sheets and towels and stuff. I also paid the produce delivery service more to get them on my team. Money has a lot of power."

"It does, but I haven't seen you use it to anyone's disadvantage. You're a good person, Allie."

"Have you ever seen that Julia Roberts movie where she's a movie star, and she fell for the guy that ran the bookstore? Well, I feel like her."

"No, but are you saying you feel like a movie star?"

It was because of moments like these that men got their reputations for being disconnected.

"No, but there's a line in the movie that resonates with me. This is my version." She looked at him. "I'm just a girl, looking at a boy and hoping that one day he will like me for more than my money."

His fingers traced from her hip, up the curve of her waist, to her breast. "There's plenty to like, Allie." He circled it slowly until gooseflesh dotted her skin. "Why do you like me?"

She hadn't really thought about it. "I'm sure there are a lot of reasons, but the first is that you don't take any of my shit. You fight back, and that puts us on even footing. Besides, you find my wealth the least appealing thing about me."

He moved forward and pressed a gentle kiss to her lips. "Who broke your heart?"

"Who didn't? It's all in the past."

"No, tell me what he did, so I never repeat his mistake."

"The first guy made a Christmas list that started with a car and ended with an island. When I bought him a new set of golf clubs, he left me. The second guy ... we were supposed to get married until I said two words— prenuptial agreement. He packed his stuff that night."

"They didn't deserve you. They didn't fight for you. I would have."

If a heart could burst, hers did. No one had ever told her they would fight for her—never. Even if he didn't, at least she'd heard the words. Every woman needed to hear those words once in her lifetime.

"No fighting. Today is all about the love."

"Now, you're talking." He rolled over, so his body hovered above hers. Balancing on his knees, he slid his thumbs into the elastic waistband of her pants and tugged them down. "Yoga pants were the best invention ever."

"I agree." She yanked at the button of his jeans.

"Let me help." He stood at the foot of the bed, kicked off his shoes, and let his jeans drop to the floor.

Chippendale's dancer was the first thing that came to mind. She wondered if she played the song "Pony" would he be able to give her some Channing Tatum moves? He was rock solid, thick, hard, and ready. He bent over, and she glimpsed his backside, which was striptease, performer perfect.

"If you don't hurry, I'll queue up some music and ask you to dance for me."

He swiveled his hips and smiled. "You got dollars?"

She lifted on her elbows. "You got moves?"

He unwrapped the condom he'd been searching for and rolled it on his length. "I'll show you my moves."

And he did. The man had so many moves that her entire body ached. Her throat was sore from moaning. Her muscles were aching from the tension he caused when he got her to the edge and pulled back. Even her hair hurt from rubbing on the pillow as she thrashed around under his tongue.

"Please," she begged as she neared the edge again.

He moved up, the hard length of him teasing her entrance. "Making love is like making pasta sauce." He inched inside her. "It needs to simmer and cook for hours before it's ready."

"Dammit, Marco, I was ready thirty minutes ago." She clawed at his back and forced him deeper with her heels.

"Anything worth having is worth waiting for." He made love to her slowly. There wasn't an inch of her body he hadn't worshipped.

"Why are you torturing me?"

He stopped and looked down at her. His eyes were full of lust and love.

"I'm not. I'm loving you."

"Can you finish loving me soon?"

He shook his head. "I'm hooked, Allie, I don't think I'll ever stop."

But he did. Ten minutes later, he pulled the most powerful release from her. She wept with the joy of it, the relief it gave her, and the fullness in her heart. She hadn't realized how empty she'd become until Marco filled her life with everything.

Chapter 18

A week had passed, and Marco's life had turned full circle. Nothing had really changed, but everything had at the same time. He was still broke. The Soup Kitchen was still in trouble. His roommates were still pains in his ass, but he didn't see them all that often these days. He spent most of his nights sleeping next to Allie.

That first night, he kissed her and walked out of her place. He was halfway down the hall to his door when she peeked her head out and asked if he wanted to do a sleepover. There was very little sleep that night.

Everyone noticed the changes in him. His boss said his step had more pep. Lisa told him he actually looked happy. He tried to scowl at her and grumble to prove he was still his stubborn, cantankerous self, but all he did was smile.

He even gave out more warnings than tickets for small infractions.

Today, Allie left for work early. She had a staff

meeting and said she'd meet him at the Soup Kitchen that night.

When he arrived, Lisa was standing in the center of the room, surrounded by boxes of food.

"Holy hell, where did all this come from?"

"Your girlfriend found a unicorn."

He hadn't really thought about what he and Allie were, but girlfriend sounded and felt right.

"Maybe she's the unicorn."

"Don't piss her off, or you'll find the horn up your keister."

He walked around the stacks of boxes labeled with what was inside. There were cases of meat, boxes of produce, and bags of baked goods that ranged from baguettes to bagels. There were even boxes with cakes and cookies. Not homemade by Allie because there hadn't been time to bake while they worked side by side at the kitchen each night and then went straight home to fall into bed. She had quite the appetite, and he was game to keep her satisfied.

He looked toward the door that led into the dining room. "Is she here?" He hadn't seen her Porsche, but his head had been in a fog all week. She filled his every thought.

"Not yet, and since I can never get you alone, do you have a few minutes to go over the books?"

"You sure know how to ruin a day."

"The problems won't go away."

He and Lisa sat down at the desk and looked at the numbers. She had gone through Todd's list of fixes and prioritized them. The rainy season was on its way, and last year the whole place flooded. According to his lease, he was responsible for all repairs to the building. His parents were giving, but they weren't savvy with business or negotiations. The landlord refused any concessions.

"We'll figure it out. Maybe we can tarp it again." They'd covered the roof with a blue tarp that lasted until the first hailstorm.

"That's just a Band-Aid."

"Band-Aids are all I've got."

"We need more."

He glanced past her to the stacks of food that needed to be put away. "We've got food."

"It won't do us a bit of good if we have no place to serve it."

"I'll figure it out."

Lisa pushed back her chair and stood. "Just ask her. Fixing our roof would be a rounding error in her check-book. Hell, she could probably write it off as a donation."

He shook his head. "I'm not asking her. If I did, that would make me like every other man she's dated."

She turned around with her arms spread wide. "You have to choose to ask her or risk losing this. What would your mother do?"

He gritted his teeth so hard he was certain his molars would crack. "You're unfair."

"Fair doesn't feed Timmy or Holly. It doesn't give Shamus a place to thaw when his box doesn't keep out the cold. Don't let your pride weaken your resolve to do good."

"If I ask her, that will be the end of our relationship." He pointed to the boxes and said, "She's given enough. I've given enough. How much do I have to lose because of this kitchen?" His heart ached at the thought of losing the kitchen, but it became hollow at the possibility of losing her.

Would his mother truly expect him to lose his chance at love to save her dream? He couldn't honestly answer that. Somehow, there had to be a solution.

Allie walked in the back door and saw the boxes. She bounced on the balls of her feet.

"It came." She ran to Marco and threw her arms around his neck. "What do you think?"

"I think you're amazing." Though there was a smile on his face, it didn't reach his eyes.

"What's wrong?"

It had only been a week, but she'd learned to read him like a book.

"Nothing."

She stepped back and poked him in the chest. It was so funny because she was so tiny but fierce. "Don't tell me nothing. I see it in your eyes. What's wrong?"

There was no way he'd tell her, so he pointed to the boxes. "Who will put all of this away?"

She stared at him for a moment. "Are Dean and Stu coming in to help?"

"Nope, not tonight. Stu has an AA meeting, and Dean is on a date."

"A date? With whom?"

Lisa walked out of the office. "With me. Turns out, he likes a cougar."

He'd never seen Allie speechless, but she was silent as Lisa walked to the door.

Before she let it close, she turned back. "You need to decide."

Allie tore into the boxes like it was Christmas morning. "Decide what?"

"We have to figure out what's for dinner."

They spent the next thirty minutes unloading boxes. When they finished, he almost wept. For the first time in years, the shelves were full, and the refrigeration unit was stuffed so the doors almost didn't close.

"How did you commandeer this stuff?"

She stood tall or as tall as her five-foot-three frame would allow. "Turns out, I own an all you can eat resort. This week, our guests ate a lot."

"Your kitchen manager is okay with this?"

"As long as I promised not to fire him for high food cost, he was happy to order extra. Now, what are we cooking?"

"Something with a simple clean up, so as soon as the guests finish, I can take you home and show you how appreciative I am."

"Salad bar it is."

They diced and chopped until they prepped all the vegetables. Allie grilled several salmon steaks for a source of protein. Marco whipped up several peanut butter and jelly sandwiches for the kids who weren't fond of vegetables or fish.

As the crowd ate, they stood back and watched.

"Look at what you did," she said. "Your mother would be so damn proud."

"Would she?" he wondered.

He threaded his fingers through hers. "Look at what *we* did."

Chapter 19

She stood outside the kitchen and marveled at how she'd gotten to this point in her life. The journey was fascinating. About six weeks ago, she was buying a property. Little did she know that the change in her zip code would create a ripple effect bringing her frustration and joy.

How lucky was she to get pulled over by Marco rather than another officer? What were the chances that Judge Matthews would have sentenced her to community service if Marco hadn't asked for leniency?

She stared at the building with its patched walls and tattered roof. It needed so much. She wished she could write Marco a check, but that wasn't possible at this point. She'd spent her cash reserves on her house, and her remaining resources were tied up in Luxe. What money she had wouldn't make a dent in fixing the Soup Kitchen. Todd told her it would be more cost-effective to raze the building and start again, but she wasn't sure Marco would do that. He had an emotional investment in the place. Giving it up would be like having to bury his parents again.

She moved to the propped open door. Inside, she heard Lisa and Marco arguing. As soon as she entered, they stopped. Lisa grabbed her purse and stomped out.

Allie looked over her shoulder to watch Lisa yank the door of her Volkswagen Beetle open and speed off.

"Wow, what was that about?"

"Difference of opinion." He dragged his hand through his hair. Silky dark hair that she spent hours running her fingers through.

"It must have been a strong one for her to stomp out like that. Do you want to talk about it?"

"Not really. There are some things in life we can change, and others we can't. Sometimes you have full control of what happens. Then again, life can control what happens to you."

"Sounds deep." She lifted on her tiptoes and kissed him. It was a quick, chaste kiss that she hoped conveyed her support of whatever he was going through. "You know I'm here if you need anything."

He stared at her thoughtfully. "Knowing you're here helps."

She followed him into the office. He picked up a bunch of papers from his desk, placed them into a folder, and shoved them into the top drawer.

"Speaking of life and how it sometimes controls you..." She laid her timesheet on his desk and smiled. "Today is my last day of court-ordered servitude." Saying it made her heart hitch.

"Ditching me already?" He leaned back in his chair and folded his arms behind his head.

There was no way he could be serious. Marco had entered her system like a virus. In the beginning, all she wanted was to get rid of him, but now that they'd grown closer, she was happy to be infected by his affection, his sense of humor, and occasionally his crankiness. Although she had to admit, he was far less testy since he met her. Some would say it was the sex that softened his steely temper, but it was having someone to share the joys and burdens of life with.

"You're not getting rid of me that easily. I'm like a bad rash you can't cure. You made me feel like what I offer from my heart has value. That's quite an aphrodisiac."

The Soup Kitchen was kind of a friend to everyone. It was a place to gather, and a place to talk out concerns or celebrate accomplishments. People came not only for the food but also for the camaraderie.

He patted his lap, and she settled onto it without hesitation. "You have value. You've brought so much to my life over the past few weeks, Allie." His voice cracked. "I don't know how to tell you how much you mean to me."

She sank into him, letting her body mold to his. "I feel how much I mean to you. You show me with every hug and kiss you give."

He could have told her he loved her. She was fairly certain he did, but Marco didn't seem like the type of man to use those words lightly. When he said them, they would be worth gold because to be loved by Marco would make her feel wealthy in ways her money never could.

It was funny how perspective could change things. How often someone's perception of you becomes your perception of yourself. Words were like weapons; they could protect or damage.

Over the years, she'd allowed people to define her. Allowed them to determine her value. Allowed people's opinions to shape her. Those people didn't know what love was. Marco Rossi did. He sacrificed everything for people he didn't know. What would he do for those he was familiar with—those he loved?

"What's on the menu today?"

His mischievous smile meant the heavier mood had passed, and playful Marco was in the house.

His arms wrapped around her, trapping her close to him. Not that she would have moved. Her favorite place was in his arms.

"I was thinking I'd like my appetizer to be your kisses with an at home follow-up for the main course."

His fingers ran through her hair, gently tugging to pull her closer. Their bodies pressed tightly together until his lips were on hers. His tongue sought entrance, and when she opened for him, he eagerly made love to her mouth.

How was it that a single kiss from this man could make her toes curl and her heart sing?

She pulled back. "How about I be the appetizer, and you be the main course, and then you can come full circle, and I'll be dessert?"

He moved back to her lips and smiled against them. "I like the way you think."

She wrapped her arms around his neck, letting her fingers trail up and into his hair. This was so perfect.

Logically, they were incompatible, but it was their differences that made it work. And his kisses. She could want to throttle him one minute, but if he kissed her in the next, all was forgiven or forgotten. Whatever was in those kisses could solve world hunger and negotiate world peace.

They kissed for another five minutes, and when they parted, her heart nearly stopped. There was something in his expression that said he was looking at her in a way that she'd never been seen. He was seeing her from the inside out.

She stared at him for several seconds, memorizing the way the amber in his eyes glowed.

When the moment passed, she crawled off his lap and walked toward the kitchen.

"What are we cooking today?" she asked.

He walked to the refrigerator and opened the door. Thankfully, since Todd's fix, the handle hadn't come off once.

"It's your last day. I think you should choose."

She wrapped her arms around his waist. "Not my last day, just the last day I *have* to be here. From now on, it's my choice."

He raised a curious brow. "Would you have stopped coming if it had only been a week?"

"Duh, you were impossible."

"I was not."

"Were too."

They went back and forth like children for a minute

while she pulled chicken breasts from the refrigerator. "How about chicken tacos with rice and beans?"

"Sounds good."

"That's why I love you." She sucked in a breath and held it for a second. Had she meant to blurt that out? A person didn't "out" their heartfelt thoughts like it was a menu item. *Hey, Marco, how about some chicken tacos, rice, beans, and a side of my love?*

He dropped the bag of pinto beans on the counter. "You love me?"

Talk about uncomfortable. To say no would be a lie, but to say yes might be too soon. Did she love him for all that he was or all that he gave her, which was at least one amazing orgasm—sometimes two—a night.

She was being silly. She loved him. He had become as necessary as air and water in her life. No one ever dared to challenge her, but Marco did it every day. When she looked at him, she saw everything she wanted in a man. He was noble and honest, independent but inclusive, and he was sexy and sweet. He was hers ... or she hoped he was.

"I love so many things about you. How could I not love you?"

"Because I'm obstinate. I push back. I'm moody. Should I go on?"

She put down the chicken and stood before him. "Yes, you're all of those things and more." They shared another kiss until he backed away.

"You're a distraction. I've spent far too much time kissing you today, and now dinner will be late."

She pulled the instant pot from the shelf. "Use this,

and you'll save yourself an hour."

He pulled her into his arms. "I guess that means I can spend more time loving you."

Her heart did a little dance. It was a cross between a two-step and the Dougie. It floated and flipped in her chest. He hadn't said he loved her, but he said he would spend more time loving her. That was the same thing, right?

They worked side by side, making dinner. After everyone arrived, they served the meal. Timmy told her that his new favorite meal was tacos.

She watched as Marco took in the crowd. With each minute that passed, he seemed to withdraw.

"Are you okay?"

"I'm fine." He snapped out of his reverie and pasted on a smile.

No one was fine when they said they were.

She grasped his bicep and leaned into him. "Talk to me."

He shrugged. "It's nothing, really. I stand here and look at them, and all I can offer is a dinner and a place to gather. They need more. What they need are jobs, so they don't have to depend on me. This place is a blessing and a curse. It's a Band-Aid for some, and a crutch for many."

"You offer more than a meal and a place to hang out. You offer them a sense of belonging. You treat them like equals. This is a place where everyone feels like they fit in. They come because of you."

"That's nice of you to say, but what if the kitchen wasn't here? What if there wasn't anywhere else for them to go? What then? What would help them the most would be employment, but no one will hire them. Can you imagine how good they'd feel if they could take care of themselves?"

"Not everyone wants to do that. Not everyone is capable."

He nodded. "Yep, so the onus falls on me. Sometimes the weight is too heavy to bear."

"Then let me help."

He shook his head. "I don't want your money."

She laughed. "That's good because I'm not as rich as everyone thinks. Most of my resources are tied up in Luxe, except what was used to buy my home. There are other ways to help."

She considered all the positions they needed to fill. The one thing about the hospitality industry was that turnover was high. Luxe paid a fair wage, but there wasn't much opportunity for upward mobility.

She pulled out a chair and stood on it so everyone could see her. She let out a whistle that silenced the room.

"Today is my official last day of court-ordered volunteerism." There was a groan that floated across the room that made her smile. "Don't worry, though; you can't get rid of me that easily." She clapped her hands together in a Mr. Miyagi fashion, rubbing them to create magical heat. It was silly because she wasn't healing anyone with her personal touch, but she hoped what she offered would help, regardless. "I run Luxe resorts, and we need good people." She pointed around the room. "You are good people." She looked at Marco, who was shaking his head.

"Anyone who wants to work should come by my office tomorrow, and I'll do my best to find you a job."

There was a range of expressions on the surrounding faces that went from shock to hope. She jumped down from the chair and joined Marco, who stood by the kitchen wall.

"Why would you do that?"

"I don't know. Maybe it's because I love you or ... I'm batshit crazy."

"I'll go with the latter because I don't want to take the blame when tomorrow comes, and you realize you've just made the biggest mistake of your life."

Was he referring to loving him or inviting the masses to apply for jobs?

Chapter 20

She told him she loved him. No woman outside of his mother had said those words to him in his adult life. He'd heard, "I could love you if you didn't love that soup kitchen so much," but that was Beth, and she was the last real relationship he had. This thing with Allie happened so quickly it blew his mind. He could chalk it up to great sex, but it was more than that. The emotions were real. Maybe they found each other in the wrong way at the right time.

Telling her he loved her after she told him didn't seem right. He didn't want her thinking the words came easily because they didn't. When he said the words, he wanted the words to be right for her. She needed to know that he loved her for who she was and not what she had.

He was walking into the police station when his phone rang. Seeing her number made him warm all over.

"Miss me already?"

"You know I do, but I'm not looking for Marco Rossi,

the bedroom god, I'm looking for Officer Rossi. Can you find him?" Her pinched voice caused him concern.

"What's wrong?"

"You were right. I opened my mouth, and now I'm in trouble. I have a situation that's about one hundred people deep who are looking for jobs. I don't have a hundred jobs. I fear a riot is about to break out, but honestly, who would have thought this many would show up?"

"Every community has its own public broadcasting system. Word travels fast."

"Seriously, there were about thirty people at the kitchen when I made the announcement."

"I told you it wasn't a good idea."

"You did, and now I'm asking for your help. These people know you, and you know them, and I hoped that maybe you could help me weed out the crowd."

He had a mind to let her work through it herself. Sometimes the best lessons were the hardest to learn, but Allie's heart was in the right place. He wouldn't punish her for her kindness.

"I'll take my lunch now, and I'll be there in ten minutes."

He sent a message to dispatch. The Aspen police department was flexible as long as there was ample coverage. He got an immediate okay and headed toward Luxe.

When he walked in, the man at the front counter walked up to him. "Are you Officer Rossi?"

He pointed to his name tag. "That's me."

"Allie is on the thirteenth floor. Exit the elevator and take a right."

He took the elevator up, and when the doors opened, he found himself at the end of a long line of applicants. Some he recognized, but the majority he didn't know.

He moved through the line until he found the front. Sitting in her office handing out applications by the handfuls was Allie, who was arguing with a man standing behind her.

"Shut up, Julian. You don't know what you're talking about."

Sitting in a chair in the corner was her brother James, who seemed to enjoy the situation.

He pushed past the crowd blocking the entrance and knocked on the door. "I got a call about a disturbance."

"Oh, thank the gods," Julian pointed to the line of people snaking down the hallway. "Luxe can't take in every homeless person looking for a job just because Allie is sleeping with a do-gooder."

Marco wanted to laugh, but he contained the impulse. Instead, he raised his hand. "Do-gooder here at your service. If it's any consolation, I agree with you, but I also think people are people regardless of race, social standing, and sexual orientation. Maybe not you, but most of us are a paycheck or two away from being homeless." He took another look at Julian.

"I've been called a lot of things but rarely a do-gooder."

"Here's your chance to do good. Clear these people out." Julian pushed past him and disappeared into another office, slamming the door behind him.

"That signals my exit." James stood and walked to Marco. "Good to see you again. Let's get a beer soon."

There was a pause while he looked between Marco and his sister. "Since you're seeing my little sis, I think we should get to know each other better. I've got so much dirt to tell you."

Allie stood and stomped her heel on the tile floor. "Out!" She pointed to the door. "If you want to play that game, I'll do the same with Dani. There's so much she doesn't know about you."

James' eyes grew wide, and he hightailed it out of the office.

Allie moved to where he stood at the door. She stuck her head out, held up a finger and said, "Give me a minute." She tugged him inside her office by the collar of his shirt and shut the door, and then closed the blinds so they were alone.

"Oh my God. It's been like this all morning." She leaned into him and rested her head on his chest. Allie wasn't a woman who depended on anyone. She was as independent and fierce as they came, so when her vulnerable side emerged, he felt honored that she was comfortable enough to let him see it.

"Who's the do-gooder now?"

She exhaled and pushed herself closer to him. He listened as she breathed him in. Immediately her stiff shoulders relaxed. After a minute of silence where all he did was hold her, he moved back a step and thumbed up her chin. "What can I do to help, Ms. Parks?"

"First, you can kiss me."

He did. It was a long, slow kiss, the kind where he explored every texture of her mouth from her hard teeth

169

to her velvet tongue. When he pulled back, she looked like she could melt into the floor.

"Thank you for coming to my rescue."

"I will always come to your rescue, Allie. That's what boyfriends do."

She smiled. "Boyfriend. I like that."

"We can discuss the vernacular for our relationship later. Back to the matter at hand. What can I do to help?"

She moved back to her chair and took a seat. He moved behind her and leaned on the edge of her desk.

"I wore the wrong suit."

He raised a brow. "What does that have to do with anything?" Today, she dressed in a pink suit with black heels that made her three inches taller, and she looked fantastic.

She rubbed at her eyes. "It's silly, but if I'm facing adversity, I always wear my black Gucci suit." Her fingers walked up the buttons of his shirt. "It's kind of like a uniform. It gives me confidence." Her shoulders slumped forward. "I didn't think I'd need to bring out the big guns today, but that crowd is overwhelming. Half of them don't even have shoes on."

"How about we weed out the crowd with a few questions? They may not be the ones you would normally ask, but let me see what I can do."

"Thank you, Marco, I don't know what I'd do without you."

His chest puffed out in pride. He liked that she needed him. Loved that she loved him. Absolutely adored that she could be vulnerable with him.

He leaned forward and pressed a soft kiss to her lips.

"How about I get Lisa to run the dinner service tonight, and you and I hang out with a bottle of wine and a movie?"

"Officer Rossi, are you asking me on a date?"

"That ... or I'm trying to seduce you."

"Oh sir," she teased. "Haven't you figured it out yet? When I'm with you, I'm easy."

"Allie, I'll say it again, there is nothing about you that's easy, but I love a challenge."

For a moment, her expression turned less playful and softer. "Maybe you love me?" There was a lift to the last word that turned it into a question rather than a statement.

"Could be." He turned around and walked to the door. Though the crowd was whispering amongst themselves, the collective sounds buzzed through the hallway like a dull roar.

He raised his hand. "Can I have everyone's attention?"

There were dozens of shushes until the area was silent.

"Luxe Resort's didn't expect there to be so much interest."

Allie walked out of her office and stood next to him. Her eyes grew wider as she looked at the crowd that had amassed. "It's doubled since I called you," she said under her breath.

"So no one is wasting anyone's time, let's set some prerequisites."

He held up a finger. "If you can't pass a drug test

today, leave." There was a lot of grumbling, but dozens of people left.

A second finger went up. "If you don't have an ID on you that proves residency, you cannot apply for a job today." That alone took a good forty percent of applicants away.

"If you can't commit to any kind of schedule, this is not the job for you."

He continued to ask valid but pointed questions until the line was down to about thirty.

He helped her hand out the applications, and she guided the applicants to the conference room where she and Dani would do on-the-spot interviews.

"Can I see you alone," he asked. They walked to her office, where he closed the door and pulled her into his arms. "I love that you wanted to do this, but you can't save them all."

She tilted her chin to look up at him. "You try to, so why can't I?"

He cupped her cheek. "Sweetheart, it's an endless battle. There's always someone waiting to be saved, but it's impossible if they aren't interested in saving themselves." He wrapped his arms around her and set his chin on her head. "If I didn't love you so much, I'd bend you over my knee for being irresponsible."

When she pulled back and looked up at him, there was a tear running down her cheek. "You love me."

"Yep, since the day you cleaned the bathroom in stilettos and a safety-pinned skirt."

"That was my first day at the kitchen. I thought you hated me."

He shook his head. "Hating you would have been so much easier than loving you."

"But loving me is far more satisfying."

He started for the door. "I'll see you tonight. I'll bring the wine; you pick the movie."

"I'm picking a chick flick."

"Just kill me now," he teased. He didn't care what she chose. All he wanted was to snuggle up next to her and spend a night where they weren't serving dinner and doing dishes. He wanted a single night that was all about them.

Chapter 21

For the last few weeks, she'd been living on cloud ten because cloud nine wasn't enough to describe her feelings for Marco and where their relationship had gone. He truly loved her, and that was more than anyone had ever done.

In her office, she pulled on her Keds and bent over to tie the laces.

"Hello, Florence Nightingale," Julian said as he walked into the office and took a chair in front of her desk.

"You really need to get your history straight. She was a nurse. I'm..."

"A pain in the ass."

She hopped up and tapped her back end, "Yes, but it's a fine ass. What's up with you? Did you come over to give me the gloom and doom news about the state of affairs here at Luxe?"

He leaned back, laced his fingers, and set them on his

stomach. "Nope, you already know that we're hanging on by a thread."

Julian's thread meant we had millions in reserve, but all it would take was one crisis to clean that out, and we'd be mortgaging property like a Monopoly player gone bust.

"I've tugged on that thread, and it will hold us. Come next summer we'll be fine. Give it five years, and your coffers will overflow to the point you'll need dump trucks to pick up the excess." Julian was always the money man. To look at him, no one would know he grew up dirt poor. He wore a custom suit as good as any man. When they went into business, he was the perfect bean counter because he'd been doing it his whole life. He was frugal but understood the need for quality.

"How's the cop? Has he brought out his cuffs yet?"

"Why, you want to borrow a pair for your next date?"

He smiled. It was a slow lift that turned into a boyish grin. "You think he'd loan them to me?"

She walked past him and slapped him upside the head the same way she did her brother when he got out of hand. She might be younger, but with men like Julian, James, and Marco, she had to draw the line, or they would bulldoze over her.

"Don't you have beans to count? I think the White House called, and they'd like you to balance the budget."

"I wish. Do you have any idea how much fun that would be?"

"You're a sick man. Get a girlfriend."

Julian chuckled. "Why have one when I can have many?"

"Because it's cheaper than a bunch of first dates."

He rose from the chair and walked to the door. "I always go dutch on the first date, and there's rarely a second date so..."

She grabbed her bag and walked past him. "Cheap bastard." She moved down the hall toward the elevator.

"I'm frugal; there's a difference."

She lifted her hand in the air. "When you have money, there isn't much difference. You're either willing to spend it or not."

The door opened as she arrived, and James stepped out. She lifted and kissed his cheek. "Love you, brother, but you need to talk to Julian. He needs to find a girl, someone who will claim his heart and tame his behavior."

"Oh, now you're Cupid?"

She walked inside the elevator and pressed the button for the ground floor. "No, if you ask Julian, I'm Florence Nightingale."

"But she's a nurse," he said as the doors closed.

"I know, go educate him."

She was in a fabulous mood. Each day spent with Marco got better, and each night was explosive. Since their first night together, she hadn't spent another alone. Her three-foot pile of lap blankets hadn't grown. In fact, it had dwindled because she brought them to the shelter and handed them out to those who wanted them.

It was another source of pride because everyone wanted one.

Her social life could no longer be measured by the number of chain stitches she finished each night.

She practically floated on air when she entered the Soup Kitchen.

Lisa was angrily scribbling a note. She pressed the pen to the paper so hard that she tore it in places.

"Everything okay?"

Lisa looked up at her and growled something deep and throaty.

Allie was never certain where she stood with Lisa because she was friendly but often aloof.

"Do you want to talk about it?"

Lisa slammed the pen on the table. "I'm done talking."

"You haven't said a word to me, so why don't you tell me. I can't do anything if I don't know what the problem is."

Lisa rubbed her hand over her face. Allie saw that her knuckles were bloody and abraded.

"Oh my God, did you get into a fight?" She went straight for the first aid kit.

"Yes, I had a fight with the breaker box. It's rusted shut."

"I'm sorry. Here, let me help." Allie pulled out a sanitizer wipe and dabbed at the cuts on Lisa's hand.

"You wanna help?" She yanked her hand back. "Write a damn check. Lord knows you've got the money."

Everything in her body tensed. It was a familiar feeling, a chill that seemed to freeze her from the inside out.

"Are you saying my only value to the kitchen is my ability to write a check?"

Lisa frowned. "All I'm saying is anyone can lend a hand, but you could really help if you wanted."

"I am helping; I show up. My resort donates food. My employees have been here to help with minor repairs."

Lisa opened the drawer and slapped the report on the table. "Have you seen this? Come July, when the rains start, we'll be walking in inches of water. The stove doesn't light because it's old and a piece of shit. The plumbing is patched together with glue and tape. Don't get me started on the heating. You've never been here in the winter, but it isn't pretty. Marco sets up space heaters, so no one freezes to death."

"I had no idea."

"You wouldn't because he won't tell you." She rose from her chair and stomped toward the door. "I've got to get olive oil from the store."

Allie reached for her purse. "Here, let me pay for it."

Lisa shook her head. "Nope, apparently, your money isn't good enough for us." She walked out and slammed the door behind her.

She sat in the chair and stared at the lengthy list. Her experience with building resorts gave her deeper insight into expenses, and Lisa was right. This list could drive a person into bankruptcy.

The roof alone would take thousands. The inside needed to be gutted and started over.

Her old insecurities went to work, making her question everything. Had this been Marco's endgame? To make her fall in love with him and then ask her for money.

The thought was ludicrous. They'd had plenty of conversations about money and never once had he asked her for anything.

Maybe that was his plan. Was she supposed to feel guilty enough to write a check? She did. Her conscience was ready to put pen to paper right then.

Instead, she started dicing onions for the meatloaf on the schedule. She'd moved on to dicing potatoes when he arrived.

He walked straight to her and pulled her in for a hug and kiss. She unconsciously stiffened in his arms.

He pulled back and frowned. "What's wrong?"

She dropped the knife to the stainless-steel table. "You tell me?"

"I've got no idea what you're talking about."

She marched into the office to snatch Lisa's note from the desk. Scribbled across the top, it read,

Ask her for the damn money.

A deep grumble filled the air. "She had no business writing this."

"Tell me how much you need."

He went to the sink to wash his hands. "I don't need anything." He took over dicing the potatoes.

"You're lying. I've seen the list. You need everything."

"It's not your problem."

"Being with you makes it my problem."

"Not true. I don't want your money."

"But you *need* my money."

He stopped slicing and put his hands on her shoulders. "Allie, drop it. I wouldn't take anything you offered."

Hurt seared her insides. "You seem to take everything I offer each night." Her voice pitched louder. "You're not turning me down when I let you into my bed."

"This is different."

His body language said this wasn't a talk he wanted to have. He grew in front of her, which meant he felt vulnerable. Just like a dog whose hackles raised, he transformed into something intimidating, but he didn't scare her.

She poked at his chest. "No, it isn't."

A breath whooshed from him. The action brought him back to his normal height. "Yes, it is because you give your body to me freely, whereas you'd never offer your wealth."

She stood in front of him dumbfounded. Her internal instincts took over, and her mouth ran on autopilot.

"It always comes down to money."

"No, it doesn't. I've never asked you for a dime, but you'll make this about money, and that's on you."

"You can be such an asshole." She walked to the desk, picked up her purse, and made her way to the back door.

"So, you've said."

"I can't be with someone who isn't honest with me. If you needed my money, all you had to do was ask."

He shook his head with an incredulous look across his face. "You can't have it both ways, baby. You can't love me for not wanting your money, and hate me because I could use it, and never asked for it."

"You could have asked."

"I would never ask. Believe it or not, I listened to you. I heard you when you spoke about the other men in your life and what they valued. I was never after your money, Allie. All I wanted was your love."

Her heart nearly broke looking at him and the hurt in his eyes. "I'm sorry."

He forced a smile to his lips. "So am I." He looked around the kitchen. "I've got the rest of this. Why don't you head home?"

Had he dismissed her?

She walked out the door and climbed inside her SUV while tears stung her eyes and spilled down her cheeks.

She didn't know how she got home; she must have driven in a daze. One minute she was crying in the parking lot of the Soup Kitchen, and the next, she was in her parking spot at Evergreen.

She went straight for the wine sitting on the counter. She didn't even bother with a glass; she uncorked it and drank straight from the bottle.

The *Recipes for Love* book sat in front of her. She turned it to Passion Pillow Cookies and cried more. How was she supposed to figure out love when even her cookies fell flat? On the bottom of the page, she read the note again. *Turn the page if you give up.*

She threw her hands up and yelled. "I do. I freaking give up."

When she lowered her hands, the disruption in the air lifted the page, and she read what she refused to earlier.

Dear Baker,

Never give up on love. I didn't tell you what to fill your cookies with because we are all looking for something different.

Pillow cookies are like people. They can dress the same

and act the same, but inside they are all different. A cookie, like a person, can look perfect on the surface, but inside, it might be a mess. Since you turned the page, I'm thinking you've created a mess or two yourself.

Allie sniffled and took another swig of wine. "Got that right."

Don't fret. You can always change what's filling your cookie and your heart. Dig deep inside, and you might realize that the answer is as simple as filling your heart with love.

Don't give up on love.

Adelaide Phelps

She lifted her hands in the air. "What in the hell do I put in the cookies?"

She heard Marco's voice in her head. "Not everything has to be hard."

"That's it! Jam. It's as easy as jam. It's what's on the inside that counts." She rose from her seat and gathered the ingredients. "I'm so damn stubborn. Marco is the jam inside my cookie. He's sweet and hot and the perfect ingredient in my recipe for love."

He wouldn't come to her that night. Even if she asked him to, he'd give her the space she needed to think and make decisions. That was who he was. She'd pay him the same respect.

She considered everything about them while she baked. When they were together, they were perfect because the ingredient she missed in her life was love. Love of self, love of humanity, love of Marco. To love someone fully, you had to look deeper. You had to see the jam filling them and appreciate its sweetness along with everything else.

Tomorrow, she'd let him know, not in words, but in deeds.

Chapter 22

Marco was a bear of a man all day. He'd ticketed three people before noon. Normally he'd listen to their excuses, but he didn't have the patience. Exhaustion consumed him. He was so damn tired of everything. He sat in the parking lot of the Soup Kitchen with his head resting on the steering wheel.

He hadn't slept the night before. He tossed and turned as his mind relived his argument with Allie. It was such a stupid fight. They were both on the same side, but it didn't feel that way. He would not ask her for money. Her love was far more valuable to him.

Somewhere deep inside, she loved him enough to give it to him, but he wanted to be different from the other men who had once loved her.

Hell, he was a man who truly loved her. They couldn't have felt the same if they left her.

He pounded his head gently against the leather-wrapped steering wheel. "Stupid. You're so stupid. You pushed her away. You dismissed her like she had no value." To his left sat her Porsche. He hadn't noticed she was already there.

His heart picked up its pace. It had to mean something that she came back. He opened the door and almost ran inside.

Was she there out of loyalty to his patrons or love for him?

"You'll never know if you don't go inside." He held the door handle and took a few deep breaths before he swung it open.

The back room was empty, but there was music floating through the door that led to the dining room.

He drifted to it and peeked through the crack to see Allie place fresh flowers on the center of a table. She had transformed his dining room from something that looked like his mom's kitchen to The Lodge at Luxe minus the chandeliers. He pushed through the door.

She stopped and stared at him. They both took each other in for a long minute before they moved closer to each other.

How was it that being away from her for a night felt like a lifetime?

"I'm sorry," she said before she threw herself into his arms.

"No, it was me. I was an asshole."

"Why? Because you loved me? Because you treated me like I wanted to be treated? Because you valued who I was and not what I could have offered?"

"No, because I dismissed you like you weren't important. You are Allie. You're the best thing that ever happened to me."

She raised her hands like a kid, and he lifted her until she wrapped her legs around his waist. She kissed him with the same desperation he felt. Like he was a starving man, and her kiss was the food he craved. The only thing that would satisfy his hunger was her.

They stood there in the middle of the dining room and kissed like teenagers on their first date. When they parted for a breath, he held her tightly to his chest. If he had been able to, he would have asked her to climb inside him, so he was never without her again.

"I love you, Allie."

"I love you too." She slid down his body but continued to cling to him. "You're the jam in my cookie."

He laughed. "What does that mean?"

"You'll see." She turned around, so her back was to his front. "What do you think?"

"I don't know what to think. Where am I?"

"You're home, but tonight is special. Tonight, we celebrate what love means. It doesn't have a price tag attached. Why can't everyone dine like kings occasionally?"

"Or queens?" He looked at the cloth-covered tables. The wine glasses and the silverware that weren't here yesterday glistened on the white tablecloths like highly buffed gems. "You're nuts, but I love you. Tell me what we're cooking, and I'll get it started."

"We're not. The Lodge is catering tonight's meal. It's a new three-course dinner." She wrinkled her nose. "No wild game."

"Not a fan?"

She shook her head. "Nope, the only wild I want is

you in our bed tonight if you're game." She tilted her head up and waggled her brows.

"I'd like that. I missed you."

"I learned a lot last night by being alone."

"Oh yeah? Tell me."

She leaned into him. "I don't like being alone."

"Since we don't have to cook, do you want to go into the office and make out?"

She took a step forward. "If the food doesn't arrive soon, we might have to cook. Let me call Flynn and see what's up."

He followed her to his desk while she dialed the chef at Luxe.

"Molly, can I speak to Flynn?" She frowned. "Okay, tell him to call me because the foods not here."

Just as she hung up, a knock sounded at the back door.

"I bet that's the food," he said.

He opened it to find a full wait staff.

He turned back toward Allie, who was digging into her purse. She whipped out a handful of bills.

"What are you doing? We could have served."

"Tonight is about us and our love for each other. Our love for the people you help. Our love of food. Tonight, we dine." She nodded toward the staff. "They serve." She walked to each of them and handed them a hundred-dollar bill. She twisted around to face him. "Before you say anything, this is important to me. We can talk about the repairs needed on the Soup Kitchen later, but this helps many people."

She pointed to the dining room and told the five waiters to finish setting up.

He watched as they moved away and pulled her back into his arms. "You're crazy."

"Yep, I've been told. Anyway, as long as the food arrives, it should be a blast."

"Where do you think the food is?" Just then, another knock sounded at the door.

"I'd say it's here." She ran to open the door. A kid with a Luxe name tag that said Darwin stood there looking sheepish. "Sorry I'm late. I ... well, I ran out of gas, but I'm here. Can you tell me where to put the bins?"

"You're two hours late. My dinner better not be ruined," Allie said.

"It should be fine. Flynn said to put it in warming drawers to keep it hot."

Allie looked at him and laughed. "Warming drawers? That's funny, but we can add that to the list."

Marco wouldn't tell her that there wasn't a list for dreams. It didn't matter what she planned to do; he'd still never ask her for money. He would continue to fight for the Soup Kitchen. It would stay open until the last grain of rice disappeared. Loyalty and service were ingrained into his being, but he'd never ask her to foot that bill.

Darwin brought in the first bin. "I'd say let's toss the main course into the oven to get it hot."

Marco asked, "How long has this stuff been in the back of your truck?"

"Not long, and the cold stuff is on ice."

They helped him carry in the bins and put the hot dishes in the oven. The kid moved around the kitchen like he owned it, and tonight, he did. He pulled dishes from a box and started plating the first course, which looked like a fancy salad with beets and goat cheese. They set aside several plates and arranged the vegetable sticks with ranch dressing next to the fresh fruit.

"Those are for the kids," Allie said. They watched Darwin carve mini apples to look like swans and filled the backs with yogurt.

"We are no longer needed here." She yanked at his arm and pulled him into the office where she loved on him until they served dinner.

He'd never seen the Soup Kitchen look so elegant or its patrons look so proud to be dining in this fine establishment. The waitstaff treated each one like they were VIPs.

Allie didn't bring the fancy stuff for any reason other than to prove they were equals. It wasn't the amount of money in a person's account that gave them value, but what was in their heart.

After the salad came the main course, which was organic chimichurri chicken breasts served with fingerling potatoes. She kept the menu simple to fit the needs of everyone. It was delicious and looked so fancy on the plate. All the colors were there from the white chicken to the red potatoes and bright green asparagus topped with yellow hollandaise sauce. Dessert was a sampler plate with petit fours, chocolate truffles, and a cookie stuffed with jam.

He held up the powdered-sugar-coated cookie. "Now, this is a pillow cookie." He took a bite and hummed. "It's perfect. Maybe you can ask Flynn how he did these."

She leaned into his shoulder. "I don't have to; I made them myself."

His eyes grew wide. "Wow, what did you fill them with?"

She looked up at him. "Love." She giggled. "Or jam. It was that easy. Turns out, it's what's on the inside that counts."

He kissed the top of her head. "It always has been."

———

AFTER THE KITCHEN CLOSED, they went home and made love. Lying in each other's arms felt right until Allie jumped from the bed and raced to the bathroom to throw up. Fifteen minutes later, they were taking turns.

When Marco's phone lit up with messages about others being ill, they knew they were in big trouble. With several seeking medical help from the emergency room, it would only be a matter of time before the health department investigated, and that meant doom for both Luxe and the Soup Kitchen.

Chapter 23

When the phone call from Susan Horton came in asking if they could come to the hospital, Allie's heart stilled. She didn't have any details, just that they needed to come right then. Despite feeling like hell, there was no way they weren't going.

Pale and looking like death warmed over, they walked hand in hand into the hospital emergency room.

They arrived at the front desk, but before they could say a word, the nurse called over her back. Two more coming in.

"Soup Kitchen?" she asked.

Marco's shoulders sagged, and he nodded, but Allie had learned long ago that you didn't feed yourself to hungry prey.

"What about the Soup Kitchen?"

"It's where ninety percent of our cases are coming from. Seems to me that it's easy to deduce where all these people got sick. Lucky us ... not one of them is insured."

Allie's hackles rose. She hated the state of affairs for the people who ate at the kitchen. Being insured was the least of their problems. Feeling responsible, she reached into her bag and took out her credit card. "Now they are. If they ate in the Soup Kitchen and are here to seek medical treatment, I want them treated with the same respect any paying person would get."

The nurse took offense. "We treat all of our patients the same."

"Oh, lucky us," Allie tossed back.

Bile rose to her throat, and she raced to a nearby trash can to heave.

Marco was right behind her, rubbing her back. "You okay, honey?"

She used her grip on the can to stand taller. "No. I'm pissed off. Just because Susan or Dean or anyone else doesn't have money doesn't mean we should treat them like they're less than anyone else."

He pulled her into his arms. "I agree, but that's not how the world works."

"The world is sicker than we are." She marched back to the window. "We are here for Susan Horton."

The nurse whose name tag showed Amanda searched through her logs. "Are you family?"

Marco shook his head. "No," he started, but Allie touched his arm. "I'm her sister Allie. She didn't get to tell me what was wrong but told me to come right away. I'm assuming the kids are sick?"

Looking bored, Amanda shook her head. "Privacy act … she needs to tell you herself." She pointed to the door and pressed the button.

She and Marco bolted to open the door before the buzzing stopped. "Bed eighteen," Amanda called after them.

As they passed the occupied beds, they saw many familiar faces.

"I'll be right there. I need to check in on the others." He held her eyes for a moment. In them, she saw concern and sadness—mostly sadness.

"Tell them not to worry about the bill; it's taken care of."

"You shouldn't have done that. That simple but kind gesture is like admitting guilt."

"What's not to admit? I catered dinner, and all these people are sick. I'd say it's my responsibility to care for them."

He cupped her cheek. "You don't know that. It could have been the water. We've been having so many plumbing problems lately, maybe that's where the problem lies."

She shook her head. "I know you don't want me to feel bad, but I already do. There's that saying, 'No good deed goes unpunished.' This is my fault, and I'll take responsibility for it."

He cupped her cheek. "Let's talk about this later. Go see Susan. I'll be there in a minute."

When she reached bed eighteen, she took in a deep breath. What would she find behind the curtain? Most of the beds were filled with occupants who had IV drips. It would gut her if little Blythe, Holly, or Timmy were attached to tubes and monitors. She wouldn't feel much better if it were Susan, but at least she was an adult and had the emotional capacity to deal with it.

Tears pricked at her eyes just thinking about those beautiful babies suffering.

She peeled back the opening to the curtain and walked in. Susan lay on the bed hooked to the IV with Blythe cradled in her arms while Holly and Timmy slept together in a nearby chair. They curled around each other like kittens trying to find warmth.

It both warmed her and broke her heart to see what she'd done to this family.

Susan opened her eyes and gave her a weak smile. Allie rushed to the bed and took a seat on the edge. "I'm so sorry." The tears spilled from her eyes, running down her cheeks to drip on the white sheets.

Susan lifted her shaky hand to touch Allie's arm. "No need to be sorry. These things happen."

Allie shook her head. "Not to me, they don't."

Susan attempted a laugh, but it sounded more like she was choking. "Welcome to my world."

Allie looked down at Blythe, who burrowed into the blankets next to her mom. She was just a baby. Her life should be filled with hope and opportunity, but if they stayed in the same situation, Blythe's, Holly's and Timmy's futures didn't look promising.

"I'm sorry to call you guys, but I don't have anyone to look after the kids, and they said if I couldn't find someone to care for them while I'm here, they would contact social services. I never want my kids to be in foster care. Strangers won't read to Timmy every night.

They won't know that Holly is afraid of the dark and needs her blanket to fall asleep."

Allie looked at Holly, who was clutching a pink blanket that was loved so much the silky edges of the binding had frayed.

"I just poisoned you, and you want me to take your kids?"

Susan rocked her head from side to side. "When you put it like that, it doesn't sound right, but yes. The kids love you and Marco, and I was hoping you could keep them until I'm released." She patted her stomach. "Looks like the worst of it is over. I'm guessing it was the hollandaise sauce."

Allie's hand came to her mouth. "Oh my God, I think you're right." She remembered it sitting on the counter. It had been the only thing not hot or on ice when it arrived.

Marco walked inside. "Nope, it was the water." He'd heard the conversation. "That's the story the rest of us are sticking to. Some kind of microbial or bacterial infection I introduced when I patched the plumbing."

"Yes," Susan said. "The water tasted funny."

Allie shook her head. "No, that wasn't it at all."

"Get with the plan, sweetheart, or get left behind."

"But Marco, if you stick with that story, they'll shut down the kitchen."

He nodded. "Yes, but we say the food came from Luxe, it will ruin you."

Marco went over to Timmy and Holly to give them a nudge.

Timmy woke and rubbed his eyes. He sat up and pulled his sister into his arms.

The gesture brought Allie to her knees. She and James were like that as kids. He looked after her like it was his sole responsibility to make sure she was okay.

"We didn't eat the paragus," he said. "That's why sandwiches are better. I've never eaten one that made me sick."

Marco smiled. "How about going out for sandwiches with Allie and me while your mom rests?"

"Can we go to Timmy John's?"

Allie looked at Marco, and he smiled. There was no way they would tell him it was Jimmy John's. She took a sleepy Blythe and settled her into the car seat.

"Susan, we've got the kids for as long as you need." She leaned over and kissed her on the forehead. "Just rest and get better. I'm so sorry."

"Me too." She nodded toward Blythe, who stretched before she let out a cry. "She's teething."

"Wonderful," Allie said. "That sounds about as pleasant as eating wild game."

They gathered the kids and stopped by the other beds to say goodbye to those who had suffered because Luxe had failed to keep them healthy. On their way out, she visited the intake desk to get her credit card. "Make sure they get what they need." She was about to walk away, but she turned around and came back to Amanda. "It doesn't take much effort to be nice. Never forget that we are all just a paycheck or two away from needing help. Who will be there when it's your turn?"

She picked up the baby carrier and followed Marco, who had two children holding one of his hands and a car seat in the other.

They struggled for ten minutes to figure out how to put the car seat in the car. Eventually, Timmy showed them how to buckle the baby in on one side and Holly on the other. He climbed in between the two seats.

Marco looked over his shoulder and smiled. "Instant family."

Allie laughed. "Baptism by fire."

"Who wants to go to Timmy John's," Marco shouted.

The raucous noise that erupted in the back seat should have made her head explode from her shoulders, but seeing the three kids so animated and happy made her smile.

They arrived at the sandwich shop and ordered the kids' food. Allie couldn't imagine eating anything, so she sipped on Sprite.

Marco gave a chicken sub a try. Anyone looking at them wouldn't see the truth of their predicament. All they would see was a family, albeit an odd family, with a dark-headed father, a redheaded mother, and three beautiful blond-headed children.

Marco must have been thinking something similar because he looked into her eyes like he was searching her soul. "Do you want children?"

She let out a heavy sigh. "I definitely wanted children, but as I said before, I want a husband first, and now it seems like it is too late for kids." She held up her hand. "I know, I know ... a seventy-year-old woman gave birth, but at seventy, all I want to do is crochet lap blankets. What about you?"

"I definitely want kids." He looked at the three sitting with them. Blythe was in her car seat on the bench beside him. Timmy was sitting beside Allie, and Holly bounced in the highchair. "I'm not sure I'd want three. Seems to me that you should only have as many kids as you have hands."

"Your baby mama should have two hands too. I mean, she might not, but probably will."

He reached across the table and took her hands in his. "You're right." He smiled widely. "That means we can have four."

Her heart hammered in her chest. Was he talking about having children with her, or was he using the "we" as a place keeper for whoever would have his babies? She closed her eyes and thought about Marco's children. They would be adorable, chubby little babies because Marco was all about feeding everyone. They would have his eyes and hair and his smile.

Thinking about babies with Marco made her ovaries dance, but the reality of their situation stopped the music and forced her to address the crisis at hand.

"I don't want you taking the blame for the food poisoning issue. We should place blame where it belongs —on Luxe and me."

He didn't let go of her hands.

"Yes, it was probably the hollandaise sauce, but honestly, you shouldn't ever put your money on a lame horse. The kitchen is crippled beyond repair. There's no reason for Luxe to take the blame." He squeezed both of her hands. "You and I know that if it got out that the food was from Luxe, it would take a long time to recover from that. Your resort would suffer."

"But they'll close the kitchen, and your patrons will

suffer." She eyed the three kids at their table. "Who will feed them?"

"We'll figure it out."

THEY RELEASED Susan from the hospital later that day. Marco loaded the kids into the car and went to pick her up.

Allie volunteered to go with them, but there weren't enough seats in the Jeep for all of them once they got Susan. She could have followed him in her SUV, but he told her he could handle it.

Though he played at being happy for the rest of the afternoon for the kids' sake, she could see the sadness in his eyes. The Soup Kitchen was more than a place to feed the hungry. It was a place where he could be close to the memory of his parents. The Soup Kitchen, on so many levels, was home to Marco.

It broke her heart that he'd have to close it. It also filled her full of love that he'd be willing to sacrifice everything for her.

She couldn't allow him to do that, and yet, she couldn't allow Luxe to get buried by a bad reputation. Everyone's money was tied up in the success of this resort. There had to be a solution.

She glanced at her watch and called an emergency meeting. After she sent a text to Marco saying she was going into the office, she dressed in her black Gucci suit and headed to Luxe.

When she arrived, the department heads were

already gathered in the conference room, along with James, Dani, and Julian.

She stood at the end of the long table. "We are in a crisis, and I need solutions."

Chapter 24

It had been several days since he went to the Soup Kitchen to meet the health department inspector.

The man had nothing negative to say about the cleanliness of the place, but everything about the condition of the building. The plumbing and electrical were out of code. The heating and roof needed repairs that he couldn't afford.

He had watched the inspector slap a note on the door that issued a warning and a message that the kitchen would be closed until further notice. That was like a knife to his heart. Everything his mother had done was gone. Her words of wisdom would stay etched in his mind. He'd remember the feel of the wooden tables under his fingertips. The frustrating refrigerator unit and the stovetop that refused to light would become a faded memory.

He contacted the landlord and ended his lease. That was two days ago, and he still felt out of sorts. His job and the Soup Kitchen had consumed his entire life, and now he had so many hours left in his days.

Sure, he spent his nights with Allie, but she'd been busy making sure that what happened the other day never happened again. She'd instructed Flynn and Molly to do a refresher course with all their employees about safe food handling practices.

He was happy she hadn't fired the kid who delivered the meal to the kitchen. While it was his fault, Marco understood that mistakes happened.

His day job was full of watching them unfold. He sat in his car, filling out the paperwork on the last person he pulled over. He considered his position in the force. He'd always stayed a beat cop so he could run the kitchen. His dream had initially been to become a detective. The force had offered him the position many times, but the hours weren't conducive to having a night gig.

He pulled onto the highway just as a call about a disturbance came in. The address was the Soup Kitchen. He turned on his lights and headed that way.

As he traveled, he thought about his life. He and Allie stood out front the night the health department closed the kitchen and handed out gift cards for nearby restaurants. She claimed that they were donations, but he knew better. She had purchased them herself.

Thinking about her made everything better. She was the orange in the sunset and the first ray of light in his morning. She made this whole mess bearable. A lesser man would have blamed her, but it wasn't her fault.

He turned the corner and thought of his mother. She had once told him that a higher power was always sending them messages. At first, it knocked lightly, then knocked loudly, and if the recipient wasn't listening, it threw a brick through the window. The food poisoning was the brick.

He arrived at the Soup Kitchen to find an entire crew pulling the roofing material off the building. This wasn't a disturbance. Sure, it bothered him, but it was life.

Crew members moved around the property like ants.

The sight of a woman in stiletto heels and a hard hat stunned him. Since when did women wear those to install a roof? He looked closer and recognized the legs with highly defined calf muscles. He'd had those legs wrapped around his waist only that morning while he made love to her in the shower.

He climbed out of his cruiser and started the walk toward her. She stood next to a man wearing an identical hard hat. He recognized him as her brother James. As he looked around, he saw more familiar faces. Dean and Stu were picking up trash and taking it to the nearby dumpster. As he neared, he saw Timmy standing behind a counter in the doorway selling lemonade for five cents a glass.

"What's going on here?" he asked as he approached Allie and James.

"Oh," she turned around and smiled. "It's a community outreach program Luxe is sponsoring."

The emotions moved into his throat. He feared if he swallowed, he'd choke on his feelings. Instead, he pulled his tough cop persona to the surface.

"Who called in the disturbance?"

Allie smiled and raised her hand. "That would be me."

He looked at James. "Can you excuse us for a second?"

James chuckled. "Not if you're going to put her in cuffs. Sorry man, but I'd have to stay and see that."

"No cuffs."

Her brother snapped his fingers in an *oh darn* way and moved toward the crew that gutted the place faster than a group of women could empty shelves of shoes at a Macy's sale.

He placed his hand at the small of Allie's back and led her into the Soup Kitchen. He moved through the building, looking for a private place until he found the office still intact. He walked inside and closed the door.

"You understand that calling in a false report about a disturbance is against the law, right?"

"I'm sorry, officer." She looked up at him and batted her eyes. "Are you going to ticket me?"

He suppressed a laugh. God, he loved this woman more than anything.

He pulled his pad of tickets from his pocket. "Is this what you want?"

"Of course not," she cooed. She moved closer and ran her hand up his shirt. Her fingers walked the buttons until she reached the last one under his chin. "Isn't there anything else we can do?"

He chuckled. "Are you trying to bribe me?"

Her head shook back and forth. "No, I would never do that. Seems to me that a girl ... this girl should have to pay for her misdeeds. I'm guilty, Officer Rossi, and I'm at your mercy."

He moved her until her back was flush against the wall and his body molded to her curves. "You're impossible." He nipped at her lower lip.

"I've been told."

"No, Allie, you're impossible not to love. God, how did I get so damn lucky to have you?"

She lifted her shoulders. "It seems I have a thing for cops."

He brushed his lips against hers. "Any cop?"

"No, just big, sexy, grumpy ones."

He covered her mouth with his. While he wanted to know what all this meant, his need to kiss her was stronger.

They didn't stop kissing until a soft knock at the door sounded, and Timmy's little voice said, "I brought you lemonade. Mommy says you're probably out of spit by now."

Allie couldn't control her laughter. She squirmed out of Marco's hold and opened the door.

"I'm so thirsty. You are my hero today." She held out her hand toward Marco. "Give me a quarter."

Marco fished in his pocket for change and handed the handful of coins to Timmy, who raced away yelling, "I'm rich."

Allie closed the door and took a seat at the desk and pointed to the folding chair in front. "Have a seat."

He did as she asked. "Do you want to explain what's going on here?"

She sipped the lemonade and set the cup on the desk.

"Yep." She set her elbows on the table and then rested her chin on her clasped hands. "Turns out that Luxe has set up a nonprofit." She lifted her head and spread her hands out as if to say look around you. "We got this place cheap because it was falling down around the edges." She opened the drawer and pulled out a folder. "This is the plan for Mama's Kitchen."

She sucked the air straight from his lungs. "Mama's Kitchen?" He wasn't a man who cried, but he felt the emotions welling up inside of him. "You're reopening the kitchen?"

She nodded. "Yes, but with some changes. It will be a community kitchen. Those that can pay will pay what they can afford. Those that can't pay will help like they do now. Lisa and Susan will run it and be paid for their time. You can help as little or as much as you want, but I'd like to reserve a few nights alone where it's just you and me."

"Are you asking me out on another date?"

Her eyes rolled up to look at the ceiling. "You are the worse date ever. Who gets up and leaves their date alone at a table?"

"At least I paid."

"Yes, you paid for our free dinner. I left the money for a tip."

"Nice tip." He took her hand and forced her to stand before he pulled her onto his lap.

"I'm generous with other people's money."

He cupped her cheek. "You're generous with your own."

"Says the man who hates rich people."

"I was an asshole to you at the beginning."

"Yes, but you're a lovable asshole." She pressed a kiss to his lips. "Now get back to work, Officer Rossi. Aspen is safer with you on the streets."

Hand in hand, they walked out the door. "See you at home tonight?"

"I'll be there." He said goodbye to the crew and James. As he drove away, he considered how damn lucky he was to have pulled her over. He thought about his mom and how proud she would be. "You are a Rossi, she would always tell him, and there's nothing we can't do."

There was no doubt his mother would have fallen in love with Allie. She wasn't Italian, but Mama would have gotten over that as soon as she looked inside Allie's heart.

The rest of the day, he thought about her and their life together. They were opposites. She was Gucci, and he was Walmart. She was caviar, and he was grilled cheese. But there was something there from the beginning. He was a candle, and she was the flame. She lit him up in ways he couldn't deny. She was beautiful and kind and had the biggest heart he'd ever met next to his mother's. Allie was wrong for him in so many ways, which made her perfect. She was soft where he was hard, jagged where he was smooth, warm where he was cold. They fit together like intertwined fingers.

He knew right then she was the only one for him. As he made his way through town, he formulated a plan. Allie wasn't the only one who could change lives.

Chapter 25

Allie sat at her desk with the *Recipes for Love* cookbook in front of her. She'd reread the preface and the Passion Pillow Cookie recipe twice. Now it was time to finish and pass the book on.

She read the note at the bottom of the second page. It told her to jot down what she'd learned or a few words of wisdom on a new page and put it in an envelope for the next baker, then sign the last page, and secretly pass the book to someone in need.

She wasn't sure how she was supposed to know who needed it. She'd considered giving it to her head of security, but Paul was overweight and trying to lose several pounds, so he could gain the confidence to ask Marla from the gift shop on a date. This cookbook was about finding love, not sabotaging it.

She pulled a piece of paper from her desk and wrote what she'd learned from the cookbook. She opened the envelope and took the last user's message out.

Listen with your heart when your mind is confused.

Danielle

She pulled the note to her chest. Dani had been so perfect for James and for her. Good for James because he was truly in love with her, and good for her because Dani made her stop and take stock of her life. It was Dani's idea to set up the nonprofit.

Julian grumbled about it for minutes until she reminded him that it would be a tax write-off. When he saw the numbers, he was fully on board. Donating to the food kitchen made the all-inclusive slightly more profitable. He'd left the conference room that night thinking about opening food kitchens in all the cities where they had properties. For Julian, it wasn't a philanthropic pursuit but a way to pay fewer taxes and increase the bottom line.

She tucked Dani's note inside her desk drawer. She put hers in the envelope and closed the book. Part of her wanted to hoard the recipes, but Dani was right. There was something about the book and the way her life changed the minute it came into her possession. She didn't want to jinx her luck. She was happy with Marco. He was everything she didn't know she needed.

After placing the book in her bag, she gathered her stuff and headed down to Flynn's to remind him that her birthday was coming up, and she planned to celebrate it on the grand reopening of The Lodge. Since it was her special day, she got to choose her cake.

When she got to the kitchen, she found Molly gripping the knife so hard her knuckles were white.

Flynn was in front of her. "This isn't acceptable. Uniform pieces cook evenly." He lifted a chunk of carrot that was bigger than the rest. "If the food critic got this, he or she would think sloppy kitchen—bad chef—worse sous chef. I won't let you ruin this for me. Do better. We've already been saved once. That whole food poisoning business could have destroyed us. We have to get this right, or the resort will be dead in the water. Everyone knows that it's the food that people talk about." He looked at Molly and said. "Are you listening to me? You need to up your game. This will be a make or break meal. Don't let me down."

Molly narrowed her eyes at him. "Oh, it will make or break us all right, because I quit." She took off her apron and tossed it on the counter and left.

"On that note, I'll leave. I'll pull together some resumes for you and have them on your desk in the morning." She looked around at the staff. "I just came down to tell you that I want a lemon berry mascarpone cake for my birthday." She pointed to the office. "I'll go write it down."

She wrote her order on the pad of paper sitting on Flynn's desk. It was an odd tablet with hearts lined across the top. Thinking about hearts made her consider the subject of love, and that brought her back to the recipe book in her bag.

A locker stood open. Inside it was a sticker that said *Love Always Wins*. She looked around so she wouldn't get caught and slid the book on the shelf before she closed the door. She didn't know if lockers were assigned or if taken randomly. She didn't care if the book went to a man or a woman. All she cared about was passing it on. If there was magic in the book or its recipes, then it would find its proper owner. If there wasn't anything special, then whoever it was, got a cookbook from a nice old lady and some words of wisdom from Allie.

Her phone buzzed, and she looked at the incoming message.

You're going to be late if you don't leave soon.

She tucked it back inside her bag and ran toward the garage. Tonight was the grand reopening of the soup kitchen. She'd named it Mama's Community Kitchen to honor Marco's mother.

She put her SUV in drive. She would definitely be late, so she reached for her phone but thought about how dangerous taking her eyes off the road could be. If she were late, then so be it, at least she would arrive alive.

She was halfway there when the red flashing lights lit up her rearview mirror.

"You've got to be kidding me." She pulled over and sat, waiting for the officer to approach. Marco would already be at the kitchen, so she couldn't sweet-talk him. Her only hope was if the approaching officer was Cameron or Terry. She couldn't tell because of the glare of the sun in her mirror.

The officer arrived and looked into her window.

"Evening, ma'am."

Her hand went to her heart. "Geez, you just about gave me a heart attack." She looked up into Marco's eyes. Eyes that held enough love for everyone but focused on her. He wasn't dressed in his uniform but in a suit and tie.

"I'll need you to exit the car." He pulled the door

open and offered her his hand.

They weren't alone. Cameron stood beside him and held a video camera.

"You ready, man?"

Marco breathed in and out like he was about to hyperventilate.

He dropped to one knee and held her hand.

"Allie, you're a criminal. First, you stole my breath. Then you stole my heart." He pulled a small box from his pocket. "I know it might be too soon, but life is uncertain. The only thing I know for sure is that you are everything I've been searching for my entire life, and there is no one better for me than you."

"Oh my God, are you proposing?" She dropped to her knees. She didn't care if the gravel dug into her skin or cut into her slacks. It didn't matter that she was now half a foot shorter than him and had to look up to see his eyes. This man had taken a knee for her.

"Give me a minute. I had this whole speech worked out."

Tears rolled down her cheeks. "You had me at I'll need you to exit the car." He'd clenched it at *you are everything I've been searching for my entire life*. Weren't those the words in her journal? The words she'd always wanted to hear. "Tell me again."

"How about I tell you every day that I love you? How about you marry me, and we'll get started on those four kids?"

Cameron almost dropped the camera. "Four? Man, do you have any idea how much shoes cost?"

They looked at him and said, "Quiet" in unison.

He opened a box that held a simple white gold band with a small solitaire. "Allie Parks, will you marry me?"

She nodded and said, "Yes, I will marry you."

He put the ring on her finger. "It's not as big as you deserve, but it's filled with love."

She looked at it. "It's perfect. All I want is your love."

A call came in, sending Cameron running toward his cruiser.

He tossed the camera to Marco. "Sorry, man, duty calls. You're on your own."

He looked at Allie. "I'll never be on my own again as long as I have her."

They rose from the ground and kissed. After a long minute, she tossed him the keys. "You drive, I just want to stare at my ring and my fiancé."

They arrived at Mama's Community Kitchen a few minutes later. Hand in hand, they walked inside. It was the same but different. Everything was new except for the tables and chairs. She'd always loved how they made the place feel like home.

Susan greeted them and sat them at a table in the corner. Timmy and Holly played at another table across the room. Stu and Dean brought waters and a menu.

"We have menu's now?" She hadn't been in charge of the Mama's Community Kitchen; she was just the initiator. Many people came forward to help.

Dean stood tall. "This is Mama Rossi's community kitchen. If you can afford to pay, we happily accept donations. If you can't, that's okay too. There's always something you can do to help."

Marco set his hand on top of Allie's. "My fiancée and I would like to pay today. Tomorrow we'll think about doing dishes."

At the mention of his fiancée, the room erupted into yells of congratulations.

Allie couldn't have been happier. She looked around the room and smiled. The quotes had returned; at least some of them. *There is no such thing as hunger when the heart is full* was there, but there were different ones too.

Refuse to give up until you exhaust all possibilities.

I can. I will. End of story.

Never let the things you want make you forget the things you have.

Never let a day go by without saying I love you.

She pointed to the last one. "Is that yours?"

He shook his head. "No, that was my father's." He turned to look behind him and pointed at the one that read, *I am whole because she loved me.*

"I do love you," she said.

He touched his chest above his heart. "And I am thankful for your love."

There was an empty space on one wall. She pointed at it. "What's going there?" she asked.

"That's for you to decide."

"I have a space on the wall?" She didn't know why that was such a big deal, but it meant that whatever she put there, would be read by everyone for years to come. Her words could impact a life. Words were powerful. They had the strength to tear down and build up. They could fill you with anger or love. They were used as weapons and first aid.

She sat for a moment and watched as the people came inside and took their seats. It wasn't only homeless or those in need of charity. They called it a community kitchen for a reason; all who came here as strangers might leave as friends because that was what community was about.

"Okay, don't laugh, but I want it to say, 'Be the jam in someone's cookie.'"

He laughed anyway, but she knew he got it.

They looked at the menu to see the day's offerings.

Timmy's Turkey Sandwich.

Mama's Lasagna.

Stu

She was certain it was the meal with beef and lots of veggies and potatoes but didn't want to confirm.

They ordered the lasagna, and when they finished, she took his hand and walked him outside. They leaned against the car and looked at the lit up sign.

"Do you think your mom would have liked me?"

He laughed. "No."

She turned toward him, slack-jawed. "No?"

He tugged her into his arms. "She would have loved you almost as much as I do."

"About those babies?" she asked. "Do you really want four?"

He shook his head. "No, I really want six, but I'll settle for four."

She opened the door. "Let's go home and practice."

He had her buckled up and on the road before she could take her next breath.

"I'm thinking a boy first."

She laughed. "You get what you get."

He reached over and held her hand. The diamond on her finger twinkled in the moonlight. "I got you, and that's far more than I deserve."

Next up is A Dash of Desire

Sneak Peek at A Dash of Desire

Gabrielle Mason stared at the screen in front of her.

Job Posting #103

Luxe Resorts

Sous Chef

She read the requirements. Working at Luxe was perfect. It filled two prerequisites: it would give her a paycheck and piss off her father. Both were necessary.

She filled out the application and let her finger hover over the send button for a moment. Could she do it? Should she? Rumor had it, Flynn McHale ran the food and beverage department at Luxe Resorts and working for him could be challenging. However, zero income and potentially becoming homeless were more challenging

Her heart raced; the pace, fluttering like a humming-bird on speed. When her finger touched the key, she closed her eyes and pressed send. Though her father wouldn't say a word because silence was his punishment, he'd be angry if he found out she worked for the enemy.

She slammed her computer shut and stared at Cosmo, who weaved between her legs before he jumped onto her lap.

"Hey, troublemaker." She ran her hand from his neck to his stubby tail and leaned back in her chair.

The cat climbed up her chest to sit under her chin, where he purred—a sound which was always calming to her.

"You and I are the same. We're unwanted and only loved by those who see our value from the inside out." She stroked his brown mottled fur and sighed. "I rescued you, but who will rescue me?" No savior was coming to her aid; she was all she had.

His fur was balding in several areas. "Who tossed you away, and why?" She found the cat hunkered down by the dumpster behind her apartment building a year ago. It was the day her father fired her, and she had to find somewhere cheaper to live.

Cosmo was a kitten and a survivor. With only one eye and half a tail, she didn't have the heart to overlook him, so she swept him up and took him inside. They were a pair now, forged together by commonalities. Both abandoned and in need of something. For Cosmo, it was a can of food and a warm place to sleep. For her ... she needed validation—someone who believed in her and thought she had value.

Cosmo tired of her attention and hopped off to disappear under the couch.

Her phone lit up with a message from her sister Chloe.

Don't be late to Mom's birthday party.

"Oh, shit." She bolted from the chair and dashed to her bedroom to change. If it were up to her, she'd wear jeans and a T-shirt, but that would never work with her family. They were royalty or at least acted like it. Her father was the culinary king of Aspen, Colorado, and a parent's birthday was as important as a coronation.

Once her makeup was on, she tossed back a couple of Tums and went to the deepest part of her closet where she stored the showy clothes. Dresses by Dior and Chanel. Shoes by Manolo Blahnik and Miu Miu. Dressing for family events was like lying on a bed of nails and just as agonizing. Even Cosmo hated the clothes. The one and only time he pooped outside his litter box was at Christmas last year when she stored a pair of boots her mother bought her in the back of the closet and Cosmo climbed inside and did his business.

Today, she chose a black and white Chanel dress and paired it with black pumps. Her toes ached before she even slid them on.

The ping of her phone sounded again.

Don't forget to bring a dessert.

"Damn it." She was already late, and now she needed to get something sweet—a dessert her mother expected her to make. If she hadn't been looking for a job, she might have remembered the entire affair, but destitution had a way of turning her mind to mush.

She picked up her keys and her patchwork, bohemian bag. There was no doubt she'd have to listen to a litany of reasons she shouldn't mix couture with crap, but there wasn't time to dig out the Kate Spade handbag and switch everything over.

She rushed outside, climbed into her beat-up Jeep, hoping it would start. The alternator was on its last leg, and today was not the day for it to give out. She held her breath and turned the key, and the SUV choked and sputtered to life before it died. "Come on. Not today." She did it again and it coughed up a cloud of smoke before starting.

It was a far cry from the new Lexus she used to drive, but desperate times required desperate actions, and selling the car was the responsible thing to do.

A glance at her phone drew a growl. She was ten minutes late, but Baby Cakes was on the way, and hopefully, they had those cherry-filled cupcakes Mom loved. If they didn't, she was in deep shit.

Double-parked, she ran from the car into the shop and asked for a half dozen mixed treats and one cherries jubilee cupcake. By the time she returned, a ticket was on her windshield.

"You've got to be kidding me, I was only in there a few minutes." There was no one to hear her complain. Asking what else could go wrong was on the tip of her tongue, but she learned long ago that borrowing trouble was a terrible idea.

She tossed the ticket on the seat next to the bakery box and sped off toward calamity.

By the time she reached her parents' estate, thirty minutes had passed. She spent an additional three taking deep breaths and swallowing a few more antacids.

After pasting on a smile, she grabbed her bag, the box, and made her way to the big, round-topped wooden doors with iron embellishments more suited for a castle than a family residence.

She hadn't been back home since the fallout and wasn't sure about the correct protocol for a banished child? Did she walk inside or knock? Erring on the side of caution, she rang the bell, and Beethoven's 5th announced her arrival.

Might as well announce that I'm late with flair.

The door swung open, and Mira, the housekeeper, stood there with a smile on her face. "Gabby, it's so good to see you. Why didn't you walk in? You're family."

Gabby tilted her head to the side and wrinkled her nose. "Sure I am." She thrust the box toward Mira. "Would you mind putting these on a plate?"

Mira looked at the box and shook her head. "This won't go over well. You're a talented chef, and you brought store-bought?"

Straightening her spine, she walked inside. "No worry there. I'm as welcome as a fox in a chicken coop. No one will care what I brought."

The housekeeper hugged the box to her side with one hand and reached up to brush lint off the shoulder of Gabby's dress with the other. "They are in the living room enjoying a cocktail."

"Thank you, Mira. It's good to see you." The older woman with gray hair and jade-colored eyes nodded. She'd been with the family for as long as Gabby could remember. It was Mira that cleaned her scraped knees and applied themed Band-Aids when she was a child. She was the one waiting at home with milk and cookies after school and stayed up at night to make sure *her girls* got home safely. Her mother and father's only contribution to their children's upbringing was DNA.

"You're welcome, sweetie." She kissed Gabby's cheek. "I've missed you."

Gabby touched her chest above her heart. "You're always right here."

The *click-clack* of her heels rang out on the marble flooring of the large foyer. If it wasn't her mother's birthday, she'd never step foot in the lion's den again.

As she neared the living room, her family's voices grew louder. Chloe and Dad talked about food festival strategy while mom chatted with Aunt Celia about the new boutique downtown that carried vintage Dior.

"Hello, family." Gabby moved forward, slinging her bag behind her back, so the patchwork leather didn't draw attention. She shouldn't worry, but it was ingrained in her to care what people thought—a trait she tried to leave behind when she walked away, but old habits were hard to break. Her entire life was about pleasing others from the clothes she wore to the food she prepared.

Her mother rose from the settee and met her halfway to give her an air kiss on both cheeks.

"I didn't think you'd come."

"It's your birthday, Mom, and I'd never miss it."

Mom leaned in and whispered. "You didn't show up for your father's birthday."

"No one invited me." The heat of her father's glare sizzled her skin. It was like he'd tossed her into the fryer basket and let her sink to the bottom of the boiling oil like the discarded and useless pieces.

Chloe's feet turned toward Gabby, but she remained cemented to the floor next to their father.

"You're late," her father bellowed.

Gabby inclined her head. "My apologies. I got caught up with something." Looking for a job took precedence over getting dressed and playing with a family who never played fair.

Her father took a menacing step toward her and stopped. "What could be more important than attending your mother's birthday?"

"Oh, leave her alone." Her mother waved a hand in the air. Her enormous diamond caught the light and painted the walls with sparkling color. "It's my birthday, and I'm happy she came." Mom walked to the bar and picked up a wine glass and a tumbler. She held them up. "Cabernet or something stronger?"

"Wine is fine." But liquor is quicker, and what she needed was numbness. However, she wasn't good at holding back when she was drunk, so she stuck with the wine. She'd sip the single glass through the painful experience of having dinner at home.

As she reached for the cabernet, her bag fell from her shoulder to her outstretched arm. It swung like a pendulum for all to see.

"Oh dear," Chloe eyed the purse. "Yikes." She looked from their mom to the purse and to their mom again, whose nose scrunched up like she'd smelled meat past its prime.

"What? I like this purse. It's me."

Her father chuckled. "Yep, nothing solid, just a bunch of pieces haphazardly put together."

"They say variety is the spice of life." She pulled her bag to her shoulder and squeezed it to her side. "Besides, it's colorful and fun."

"Fun doesn't pay the bills."

"Dinner is ready," Mira said from the dining room.

Everyone walked past her to their seats except Gabby, who was displaced from her usual chair beside her father by her sister. Now relegated to a place farther down the table, she took the seat across from Aunt Celia.

"How are you?" Aunt Celia asked.

"You know, living the dream." If anyone told her a year ago that she'd be living in an apartment with a half-blind cat, she would have said they were crazy. She was a sous chef to Michael Mason and had worked at La Grande Mason, the flagship restaurant of their family. La Petite Mason should have been hers, but her moral compass was her downfall.

The five-course birthday meal took two hours, which felt more like days. Throughout dinner, Chloe glanced her way several times, and her eyes said everything her lips couldn't. *I'm sorry. I miss you. This is an impossible situation.*

It was Gabby's hope that she conveyed her message loud and clear. *Get out while you can.*

Mira served dessert on a large tray that contained several of Mom's favorite treats like macarons, no doubt made by Chloe, who was as good with desserts as she was everything else. The lemon bars were an Aunt Celia staple, while the cupcakes she bought looked like orphans on the platter.

"Who made the cupcakes?" Mom asked.

Gabby sighed. "Baby Cakes. You know, I'm not a baker, and I ran out of time. The job market has been tough. People aren't hiring chefs with the last name Mason anymore." Ever since she refused to steal a key ingredient from one of her father's competitors at the Aspen Food Festival, he fired her, and had her blacklisted from being hired at local restaurants.

Falcone's took the top prize last year with black Périgord truffle dumplings, which couldn't have happened if the truffles went missing. Their win sent La Grande Mason to second place. There wasn't any place worthy but first in her father's book, and he'd do whatever it took to make sure he got there and stayed there. She said a silent thank you to the universe for not having to take part in the Aspen Food Festival this year.

She reached into the tiny pocket of her dress, pulled out several Tums, and stuck them in her mouth. Dinner with the Masons was ulcer-inducing.

Dad's beefy hands slapped the table, shaking the silverware. "There's good news to announce." He rubbed his palms together. "I sold your grandparents' flat for a tidy sum. Just the one they lived in, not the other place where the cops live. However, the buyer from your grandparents' flat wants first dibs on the other when it becomes available, which should be in another year. I think we can get a pretty penny for that one too." He leaned back. "Your grandparents left the property to you girls, so you'll get the profits." His voice told her he wasn't happy about the arrangement, but Dad got the restaurants and the family estate along with a mountain of money when Grandpa died.

Gabby sat up. This news might be worth coming home for. "Grandma left us her property?" Grandma Mason outlived Grandpa by a year, but they were both major influences in her and Chloe's lives. Weekends at her grandparents' were like a whole summer vacation shoved into two days.

Grandpa taught them his secret recipes, even ones he never taught their father. *Everyone needs something that belongs to them alone,* he said. Her special dish was cacio e pepe, a pasta dish that looked simple but was hard to pull off.

"She did, but I'm the executor, and that means it's up to me how and when the money gets distributed."

Gabby's shoulders rolled forward like a wilted flower.

Dad was a cruel man. How someone like him could come from Fortney and Mavis Mason shocked her. Maybe it was only child syndrome. He was used to getting what he wanted when he wanted it.

"It's just over a million dollars. Half will go to Chloe now, so she can do the upgrades and run La Petite Mason." He set his hand on top of her sister's and gave it a pat. "You *will* make me proud." Why couldn't he have said, *you make me proud?* The word "*will*" changed the entire context of the sentence from a compliment to a demand.

He turned to face Gabby. "Yours is in a trust until you reach thirty-five. At thirty, you still haven't figured life out yet. It's not what you know, but who you know. It's not what you do, but how you do it."

What he meant was those who didn't fall in line got shoved out and had their inheritance held hostage. It was only a matter of time before Chloe made Michael Mason unhappy, and when that time came, she'd be gone, too. What made it worse was her sister's inheritance would sit in a restaurant she couldn't enter once he exiled her.

"That's perfect. At least I'll get it." She looked at Chloe. "Be careful how you invest your money. Make sure you have shares in the restaurant before you put any money into it."

"She doesn't need shares because she knows what loyalty means." The red in her father's face rose like mercury in a thermometer.

Certain he would explode in a nanosecond, Gabby rose from the table. "I've got to go." She rushed to her mother and kissed her cheek. "Happy Birthday, Mom. You don't look a day over thirty."

Candace Mason smiled like a pageant winner. "Thank you, darling. See you soon?"

"Sure." She wouldn't because her mother would never step into her side of town, and Gabby sure as hell wasn't coming back home. But it was her Mom's birthday, and since she didn't have money for a present, she gave her hope.

"Let me walk you out," Chloe said.

"She knows the way," her father blurted.

Chloe rolled her eyes. "I'm sure she does, but I'm walking her out, anyway."

Gabby beat her sister to the door. "Be careful."

Chloe took in a deep breath. "I'm stuck between a rock and a hard place. I see first-hand what Dad's wrath has done to you. If you can't find a job soon, you'll be behind the counter of Deep Roast, asking, 'What can I get you today? Maybe a latte, or how about a mocha?'"

Leaning in, Gabby gave her sister a hug. "Don't sell your soul to the devil."

Chloe chuckled. "Oh, honey, we're his spawn. Evil is in our blood." She looked past her and pointed to the beat-up Jeep. "That's why I'm toeing the line." Her eyes moved to the Range Rover on the other side of the circular drive. "I'm not downsizing, and I'm not down-grading."

There was two year's difference in their age and a lot more than that to separate them. Chloe was like their mother in so many ways. She loved things—expensive things, whereas Gabby wasn't the least bit materialistic.

"Don't forget the family motto," Gabby said. "It's not what you know, but who you know, and we both know our father will never change. Look at me." She pointed to herself. "Dad's a dog who's not afraid to eat his pups. Thankfully, I got out before he sharpened his teeth." She stepped back. "Watch your money and your back."

She climbed into her Jeep and prayed for it to start. When it did, she breathed a sigh of relief. Things were looking up. They had to because she was at rock bottom. She was down to the last of her savings. How many people could say they had a half-million dollars in a trust and couldn't afford to pay next month's rent?

Dear Baker

Dear Baker,

I loved writing this book because of it's message ... it's what's inside that counts. For me, at the end of the day, a person's heart will always show me what their face cannot. As for the cookies, try everything from jam to nuts. You never know what you're looking for until you find it.

Kelly

Passion Pillow Cookie Recipe

Before you begin, make sure you wash your hands because food poisoning is no joke.

Ingredients:

- 8 oz cream cheese softened
- 1 pound real butter, softened (Only use the real stuff because it's what's inside that counts.)
- 1 cup granulated sugar
- 5 cups all-purpose flour
- 1-1/2 cups jam or preserves of your choice. Or ... you can be brave and try something different like a slice of Snicker's bar. Sometimes the risks are worth the rewards.
- 1 cup powdered sugar, for dusting

Directions:

Add the cream cheese, softened butter, and the 1 cup

of granulated sugar together. Mix on medium speed until well blended.

Add the flour one cup at a time, mixing until evenly incorporated. Press dough into a ball. Wrap in plastic and allow to rest in the refrigerator for 1 hour.

Preheat the oven to 375 degrees.

Sprinkle some powdered sugar on a smooth countertop or pastry board and roll dough out into an approximately 1/4-inch thick sheet. Cut the dough into 2-inch circles. You can use the lip of a glass or a cookie cutter. In life, we have to remain flexible. Re-roll excess dough as needed.

Place 1 teaspoonful of jam or preserves or whatever else you're trying onto the center of the circle.

Wet the cookie dough edges around the filling with your finger. Place a second circle over the jam, firmly press the edges to seal in the passion. You can use a fork to make it pretty. Repeat this process until you have used up all the dough.

Place the cookies on a baking sheet lined with parchment paper and bake for 8-10 minutes or until cookies begin to brown.

Remove the tray from the oven and place on a cookie rack.

If desired, dust cookies with powdered sugar. (According to Dani, a person can't consume enough of the white stuff.)

The cookies will keep well in the freezer for long-term storage. However, they should be stored in an airtight container in the refrigerator when completely cooled.

Get a free book.

Go to www.authorkellycollins.com

Other Books by Kelly Collins

Recipes for Love

A Taste of Temptation

A Pinch of Passion

A Dash of Desire

A Cup of Compassion

A Dollop of Delight

Cross Creek Novels

Broken Hart

Fearless Hart

Guarded Hart

Reckless Hart

About the Author

International bestselling author of more than thirty novels, Kelly Collins writes with the intention of keeping love alive. Always a romantic, she blends real-life events with her vivid imagination to create characters and stories that lovers of contemporary romance, new adult, and romantic suspense will return to again and again.

For More Information
www.authorkellycollins.com
kelly@authorkellycollins.com

Printed in Great Britain
by Amazon